Three skinny socialites should be a pushover after the rough and tumble world of Wall Street. Right?

Kate Ryan may be au fait with making high-powered legal decisions, but she's about to submit to the rules of reality TV, where nothing is what it seems. Who'd have thought a few days with the cameras rolling for a low-rent cable show would be so challenging, or that the claws of a former homecoming queen, a washed-up soap star and a whiny cat-lover would be so sharp?

Books by Bernadette Walsh

Gold Coast Wives
The Devlin Witch
The Girls on Rose Hill
Cold Spring

Gold Coast Wives

Bernadette Walsh

To my husband for all his love, encouragement and technical support, and to my mother and father for always believing in me.

Foreword

Never underestimate the healing properties of an hour of bad TV and a bar of chocolate.

Chapter 1

Six months ago, I had confidence, I had security, I had a marriage. A lot can happen in six months.

Six months ago, I was a practicing lawyer and my husband, Jim Ryan, a Managing Director at a Wall Street investment bank. We were happy living the American dream in our five bedroom home on the North Shore of Long Island, tooling around in our matching BMWs. Life was good. Then Wall Street imploded.

Within weeks, Jim's investment bank dissolved into bankruptcy, taking with it not only Jim's job but our entire life savings, thanks to the leveraged investments Jim had made without my knowledge or consent. Jim was distraught, and I was distracted by my home situation, so distracted that I hadn't noticed when a younger lawyer, Martina Campbell, stole most of my clients. Since my law firm was an eat-what-you-kill kind of place, the Executive Committee fired me, and I think that was the last straw for Jim because before I knew it he had taken off for a two week trip to visit his sick grandmother in Ireland. Those two weeks became five months. Aside from a few emails, I hadn't heard from him. According to his last missive, he was in Australia.

So I had no job, no husband and a drawerful of bills when I ran into my old high school friend, Angela Mascaro Rosetti. Through her I reconnected with her brother, Chris Mascaro, a stylist for *Gold Coast Wives*, a new reality show based on Long Island. He thought I would be a perfect cast member and put me in touch with the show's producer, Elaine Rogers. She loved me, and while I didn't exactly love Elaine or the thought of exposing my personal life on TV, I did love the seventy-five thousand dollar stipend the show paid. I really felt like I had no choice. Wall Street was dead, my bank account non-existent and my monthly forty-five hundred dollar mortgage payment wasn't exactly going to pay itself. So I held my nose and dived in.

Tom, the twenty-something nose-ringed director's assistant, had called me earlier with directions to the first *Gold Coast Wives* group event, a cocktail party. The party was at the home of one of the Wives. He hadn't given me her name because Elaine didn't want us Wives to Google each other before meeting.

I carefully blew out my hair, somehow managing to tame my unruly red curls, and applied the new makeup Chris had insisted I wear. Apparently, I had appeared too ghostly in my test shots. The makeup looked darker than anything I'd ever used, but my mother and I had thought it looked okay. "It looks like you, only better," she'd said as I got ready, which I chose to take as a compliment.

Wearing one of my less boring pants suits and a pair of funky high heels I'd borrowed from my sister, I drove the BMW I'd saved from repossession through the winding roads that snaked through Huntington Bay, past the upscale sub-divisions to the ten acre estate on Lloyd Neck where the cocktail party was being held. A long driveway led to an imposing stone Tudor where three Channel 45 trucks were already parked, along with an assortment of foreign luxury cars I assumed belonged to the other Wives. Well, at least my car would fit in.

I climbed the ornate stone steps, wobbling slightly in my sister's heels. I stood on the doorstep, suddenly paralyzed with fear. Ever since I'd signed my *Gold Coast Wives* contract, I'd told myself that appearing on reality TV was no big deal, just a way to make a few bucks until Jim came to his senses, came home and somehow solved all our problems, financial and otherwise. I told myself, *hell, it's only local cable.* No one would probably see the stupid show anyway. I had numbed myself, really, unable to face what a train wreck my life had become. Me, Miss Class Valedictorian, Miss Most Likely to Succeed, had become Miss Unemployed, Miss Fat Ass, Miss Loser. But once I walked through that door there would be no turning back. If I Googled myself after today, it would not list Kathleen Griffin Ryan, Georgetown Law School Class of 1992. It would list Kate Ryan, overweight, over-forty, reality show freak. I said a quick Hail Mary and rang the doorbell. An elegant woman near my age with dark, shoulder-length hair answered the door. She looked oddly familiar.

"Hello. You must be the final Wife. It's nice to meet you. I'm Pamela Kruger."

Oh no. It couldn't be.

"Pamela Reynolds?"

"My maiden name is Reynolds." She looked at me for a moment. "I'm sorry, have we met?"

"I'm Kate Ryan or rather, Kate Griffin," I stammered. "From Queen of the Rosary Academy?"

"I attended Queen of the Rosary. I'm sorry, I don't remember you." She didn't remember pushing me off the cheerleading pyramid and breaking my ankle? The coach had called an ambulance. "I remember a Kathy with red hair. I think she became a comedienne."

"I think you mean Kathy Griffin, and she didn't go to our school. I went by Kate, and I'm a lawyer."

"How very wonderful for you. Why don't you come in and meet the rest of the girls and the husbands. Did you say you were married, Kathy? Is your husband joining us?"

"Unfortunately, no. He's traveling at the moment."

"Oh, that's too bad. Is he a lawyer too?" she asked as she led me through a marble entranceway, not seeming at all interested in my answer.

"No, he's an equities trader." Well, he *was* an equities trader.

"He might know my husband. Don does something like that." Pamela smoothed her jade green, beaded cocktail dress and led me into a living room decorated in shades of gray, blue and silver. The room was serene and soothing, almost like sitting in a cloud. "Everyone," she announced, "here's our final Wife, Kathy Griffin." The other two women stared at me since I was about forty pounds heavier and six inches taller than the real Kathy Griffin.

"Actually, my name is Kate Ryan," I said to the two women perched on matching silk teal blue chairs, also wearing stylish cocktail dresses. The three of them looked like they were attending a swanky opening or charity event--the blonde even wore an up-do. I looked like I was going to court.

"Oh, yes, sorry, my mistake," Pamela said. "Can I get you a drink, Kathy?"

"It's Kate, and yes I'll have some wine, red if you have it." And some arsenic please.

A petite bird-like woman with red, almost magenta, hair walked up to me and chirped, "I'm Rachel Finley. It's nice to see another redhead join the group. I'm usually the only one!"

I'm sorry, but if you had been called Pippi Longstocking when you wore pig tails, if you had suffered third degree burns when you went to the beach, if every time you had gone into a bar some drunk yelled *Hey Red*, then, in my book, you had the right to call yourself a redhead. But if you had become a redhead through the miracles of modern science, then you didn't. Rachel with her tawny olive skin and brown eyebrows, a redhead? I didn't think so. However, she seemed nice enough and much more interested in meeting me than Pamela, so I gave her what I hoped was a friendly smile.

"Rachel, it's wonderful to meet you too." I shook her hand and tried not to crush her tiny fingers.

"And I'm Tina Andrews," said a blond Amazon in a soft, breathy Marilyn Monroe voice.

"Camilla," I blurted as I grabbed her hand. "Oh, my God, you're Camilla Yardley from *Hope's Glen!*"

She smiled, as if she received this reaction all the time. "Yes I am. You watch the show?"

"Religiously. My college roommate was a complete addict and got me hooked."

"Why, Kathy, oh I mean, Kate," Pamela said, "how would you have time to watch a soap? I thought you said you were a lawyer."

I adopted Pamela's sour-sweet tone. "The magic of TiVo." I turned to Tina. "How long will you be in a coma?" Camilla Yardley had been in a terrible car accident after being run off the road by Miranda, a stalker obsessed with Brad, Camilla's sixth husband.

"I'm on a three month sabbatical. My agent thought it would be a good time for me to try something new. I'm reading for theatrical roles. And of course I'm looking forward to working with all of you."

Yeah, right. Who would walk away from a soap on ABC to appear on Long Island cable? According to *Soap Opera Today*--which I swear I've only read on the supermarket check-out line--*Hope's Glen*'s ratings were down and the producers had needed to fire the more expensive cast members. As a longstanding cast member, Tina probably had earned one of the higher salaries. Also, it had been rumored that there had been some tension on the set when the actor who played Brad--Tina's boyfriend in real life--had conducted a hot, not-so-secret affair with the twenty-five year old actress who played Camilla's half-sister, Raine. Okay, I used to check out SoapDish.com whenever I was on a particularly boring conference call. Sue me.

"Tina, that sounds absolutely fascinating," Pamela said. "Why don't we take our drinks and join the boys in the great room?" At first I thought Pamela was being her old alpha dog, captain of the cheerleading team, controlling self, but I soon realized it was a scripted statement because the camera men had already lined the hallway leading to the great room.

We obeyed and picked up our drinks, following Pamela and the line of cameras through the formal dining room into a great room the size of my parent's entire house. The great room, clearly her husband's domain, was decorated in hunter plaids and dark reds. Antlers hung over an enormous stone fireplace.

Three men sat in leather club chairs next to a roaring fire. A bald man rose from his chair, walked over to Pamela and gave her a perfunctory kiss on the cheek.

Pamela turned to us. "Girls, this is my husband, Don Kruger."

"Ladies," Don said in a deep baritone with a slight mid-western twang, "welcome. Let me pour you all a glass of champagne."

"This is my husband, David," Rachel said in her high, nasal Queens whine. She grabbed the heavy-set man's hand and dragged him to his feet. "David Finley, of Finley's Fine Furnishings."

"Hello," David whispered.

"Finley's on Gerard Street in Huntington?" I asked. "My husband loves window shopping there."

Rachel beamed. "Next time you just have to stop in when I'm working. We have quite the selection of furniture, fabrics, oriental rugs and lighting!"

The third remaining man smiled. He was tall with broad shoulders, mid to late fifties I thought. "Hi, I'm Paul Goodman."

"Oh, yes, this is my brother-in-law and good friend, Paul," Don said, slapping him on the back. "Sorry about that, Paul, I didn't mean to forget about you."

"Oh, you're Pamela's brother?" I asked, surprised. I had only remembered her having sisters.

"No," Pamela snapped.

"My older sister Suzanne was Don's first wife," Paul added.

"Everyone raise your glasses," Pamela said, ignoring Paul. The camera men moved in to get a close up of Pamela. "Don and I are pleased you could join us this evening. I would like to make a toast to Channel 45's first cast of *Gold Coast Wives*." We sipped the champagne. "Now," continued Pamela, "I think we should all take a moment to introduce ourselves." Hadn't we already done that?

"I'll go first. My name is Pamela Kruger. I am thirty-nine years old." Unless she had skipped three grades, she was forty-two like me. "I'm married to the most wonderful man in the world," she said with a saccharine smile, "Donald Kruger, founder and CEO of DTK Advisors." *Holy shit!* DTK was a legend on Wall Street. I couldn't believe I hadn't recognized him. "I have a beautiful six-year-old daughter, Diana, who will join us after dinner, and two wonderful stepsons. My passions, aside from my family of course," she said looking at Don who didn't seem to react, "are charity work and entertaining." She held her hand over her heart. "I believe that it is my obligation, no, it is my duty and privilege, to serve those less fortunate." And with that she gave the camera a modest little smile. Thank you, Miss America.

"Now, Rachel," said Pamela, the apparent mistress of ceremonies, "please tell us about yourself."

Rachel took a deep breath and looked into the camera. "Well, uh, my name is Rachel. Rachel, uh, Finley." She looked up at us, paralyzed with stage fright. "I'm, I'm so happy to be, you know, part of the show." Her voice broke, and her eyes teared. God, this was painful. David Finley rubbed his wife's shoulder. That seemed to calm her down.

"I was lucky enough to sit next to this lovely lady in our freshman English class at Queens College." David smiled at her.

In a stronger voice, she said, "You only sat next to me because you needed someone to cheat off of."

"I sat next to you because you were the prettiest girl in the class."

"Well, we got married the June following graduation," Rachel said, gaining confidence, "and we'll be married twenty-five years this summer."

"Congratulations," Don said. "That is a true accomplishment. My late wife Suzanne and I were married twenty-four years. Not too many people can say the same." Out of the corner of my eye, I saw Pamela shoot daggers at Don, but he seemed oblivious. He was too caught up in the Finleys' love story.

"True, Don," Rachel said, her whine reasserting itself. "Very true. Of course we have two beautiful sons. Our oldest, Nathaniel, graduated from Tufts and works with us at Finley's Fine Furnishings. He's just a wizard with numbers. Our youngest, Jonathan, is a second year med student at George Washington."

"You must be very proud," Don said. "My oldest also works with me in my business."

"We are proud. We've been so lucky in this life, what with the extraordinary success that David has made of Finley's Fine Furnishings, the premier furniture store on the North Shore. We even sell over the Internet, and there's no tax for orders outside New York." Rachel seemed to be feeling better since she was able to work in a plug. "That's why I also feel it's important to give back. My charity, LICKs, is holding its first annual charity ball in six weeks, and I would be honored if each of you would serve as chairwomen on the LICKs Charity Ball committee."

We all murmured that we would be honored, but it didn't seem as if we had much of a choice. I'd bet the invitations with our names on them were already in the mail.

"Very impressive, Rachel. What does LICKs stand for?" I asked.

"Long Island Cats and Kittens. Get it? LICKs! Isn't that cute!"

"Excuse me?"

"It's a charity for cats," Rachel explained. "Do you know how many cats and kittens are abandoned on Long Island?"

"No, how many?"

"Oh, there are so many of them," Rachel said, waving her hands. "I love kittens and cats, so I felt compelled to do something about their plight."

"Oh," I said. AIDS, hunger, homelessness, cats--I could see the connection now.

"That sounds like a very worthy cause," Pamela said, and Rachel gave her a big smile. Brother-in-law Paul winked at me. "Now, Kate," Pamela said, "why don't you tell us about yourself."

I put down my flute of champagne and cleared my throat. "My name is Kate Ryan, I'm forty-two years old. Pamela and I graduated from the same high school, Queen of the Rosary Academy, in 1985." Ha! Thirty-nine, my ass. Explain that one to old Donny. "I attended Georgetown Law School and was recently a partner at Fowler, Sherman & Potts, a New York City law firm. I'm currently on sabbatical in order to spend more time with my daughter." Hell, if Tina could be on sabbatical so could I.

"And your husband, Kate?" Pamela asked. "Where is he?"

"He's traveling."

"For work?" she pushed. I think Pamela smelled blood.

"For business and for pleasure," I countered, which wasn't an outright lie. For all I knew, Jim could have gotten a job by now: crocodile hunter, kangaroo wrestler, male stripper.

"Will he be back in time for the LICKs charity ball?" Rachel asked.

What was with all the questions? No one else had been asked this many questions. "I hope so, Rachel," I said. Again, another true statement. At least I thought it was true.

"How wonderful, Kate," Pamela said. I suspected Pammy was more than a little disappointed I hadn't fallen apart like Rachel. After ten years running hedge fund seminars, a few housewives were not about to rattle me. Brother-in-law Paul winked at me again. At least, I think he winked at me. Either that or he had some type of facial tic. I decided to go with wink and smiled back.

Pamela noticed, scowled at both of us, and then plastered on a fake smile. "Now, Tina, why don't you tell us something about yourself."

Like a pro, Tina faced the camera. Her hair, swept in an elaborate updo of which Ivana would have been proud, was platinum blond. Her cheekbones were razor sharp, through surgery or starvation I wasn't sure, and her eyes were ice blue. By far, she was the most attractive woman in the room. "My name is Tina Andrews, and since a lady never tells her age, let's just say I'm over twenty one." The men chuckled, and Pamela glared. "I'm on a temporary break from ABC's Emmy award-winning daytime drama *Hope's Glen*, where I've won two daytime Emmy awards." Okay, her producers should have been happy with that plug. "Aside from acting, which is of course a passion of mine, my other passions are yoga and step class. I believe rainbows are free, and laughter is priceless." And with that she sat down. Okay, maybe her producers wouldn't be so happy after all.

"Wonderful, Tina. Really," Pamela said. "Dinner is ready. Please join us in the dining room." Again, the camera men were a step ahead of us and preceded us to the dining room which, like the living room, was subdued yet sumptuous in a melody of grays, blues and silvers. I was seated between Don and Paul.

"Kate," Don said as we both started eating our wild greens salad, which tasted like a plate of grass to me, "I thought you looked familiar when you first walked in. I sat in on your hedge fund structuring seminar last year."

"You did? Usually only other lawyers and compliance staff took my seminars."

Don buttered an enormous piece of bread, spreading crumbs all over the table. "I like to keep up to date on all aspects of the business, to the extent that I can."

"And you didn't fall asleep during the tax discussion?"

"That was hard going, I'll admit." He laughed. He had a friendly, easy laugh. "The rest was interesting though. You even made parts of it entertaining."

"Thank you," I said, a little flustered to be receiving compliments from an icon like Don Kruger. Hell, last year he had been on the covers of both *Fortune* and *Time*. I reached for the bread. My crystal goblet tipped over with a heavy thud, spilling red wine onto the pearl gray tablecloth--it looked like a pool of blood. "Oh, oh, I'm so sorry!" I threw the matching napkin--probably not a smart move--over the stain. Paul threw his napkin over the stain as well.

"Kate, please calm down," Don said. "It's all right, nothing's broken. No harm done."

"Except to my grandmother's tablecloth. It's a family heirloom," Pamela said.

"Pamela, I'm sorry,"

"It looks like you got wine on your blouse. Why don't you go to the powder room and clean up. And you'd better check your face, something appears to be happening."

Happening? I touched my face and could feel lumps forming on my chin and across my cheeks. I shot toward the door, catching my heel on the Persian rug--probably another family heirloom. I stumbled a bit but was able to catch myself and make it to the bathroom without further mishap.

God, this was hell.

And we were only on the first course.

* * * *

The rest of the evening was fairly uneventful, except that angry red welts covered my face--it looked like I'd been attacked by a swarm of bees. Apparently Chris's makeup was not so hypoallergenic after all. When I returned home I scrubbed the makeup off my face, took four Benadryl and hoped for the best.

The next morning, I woke to the sound of rain pelting the skylight in my master bath. I felt groggy, either from the champagne or the Benadryl, and my mouth was dry. I dragged myself downstairs to the kitchen where my mother sat at the table pounding away on her Mac. "There's coffee in the pot, and I put your breakfast in the warming drawer." She didn't even look up from the screen.

Breakfast made and ready--living with the parental units conferred some advantages. Once my mother had heard about the TV show, she claimed a kitchen fire had made her home uninhabitable, despite the fact that my retired fireman father had installed the latest and greatest smoke detectors in almost every room of their small house. She'd arrived on my doorstep with her laptop, copies of her last five published romance novels and my embarrassed father in tow. Wimp that I am, I let them move in.

I took my nicely warmed plate over to the table and dug into scrambled eggs and bacon. My mother might not have liked making roasts or pies, but like most Irish mothers, she cooked a mean breakfast.

When I'd finished, she looked up. "What in God's name happened to you?"

"I had an allergic reaction to the makeup."

"During or after the party?"

"During, of course. I turned into the elephant woman at the end of the first course after I spilled red wine all over the table."

"Were you drunk?"

"Of course I wasn't drunk! I was having a nice conversation with Don Kruger, one of the best hedge fund managers alive, and I guess I was so star-struck I wasn't paying attention. Before I knew it there was red wine everywhere."

"You must have made some first impression."

"Yeah, no kidding." I scratched my cheek.

"Don't scratch. Wait, let me make you some oatmeal." My mother got up and walked to the stove.

"No, Mom. I've had enough."

"For your face, not your stomach."

"I'll take some more Benadryl." I finished my coffee.

"And you'll put this on. It will take that swelling right down. Then you can take a shower and change. You look like an unmade bed in those sweats."

"Oh, I just feel like lounging on the couch today," I said with a yawn.

"They're turning on those blasted cameras in an hour. Didn't you read your schedule?"

I knew allowing Elaine to install remote cameras in my kitchen for a more *natural feel* was a bad idea. Man, I really had to get my act together before I was fired from this gig. "Oh God, that's today?"

"Yes, and we're making brownies with your sister and the kids. Your father's gone to buy the ingredients. Thank God we're here, Kate, or you'd be thrown off that show."

"Maybe that wouldn't be such a bad thing," I moaned as my mother slapped hot, slimy oatmeal onto my face.

"Lie back and don't get any of this on my clean floor."

"Don't you mean *my* clean floor?" I mumbled.

"Quiet, madam. Now, I'll pop upstairs and change into something a little more colorful."

After ten minutes I shuffled to the sink and wiped the oatmeal off. I didn't know whether the welts looked any better, but they definitely felt less itchy. Not that I'd admit that to my mother. I'd headed up the stairs to shower and change when the doorbell rang.

"What happened to you?" Angela Rosetti said after I opened the front door. Decked out in black leather pants that screamed expensive, she was a tad overdressed. After three kids, Angela dressed as if she were in a

Whitesnake video. Lucky for her, she was still so gorgeous she could almost pull it off.

"Your brother's makeup is what happened to me."

"The LeBonne? Why, I use it all the time." Angela picked oatmeal out of my hair. "What did you do to your hair?"

"Listen, I've got to take a shower. We start taping in less than an hour."

"I know." What? Did everyone know my taping schedule except me?

"That's why I brought you some of my newest pieces." Angela shook an owl necklace at me. Angela had recently started a jewelry line. She made owl necklaces, owl earrings and owl bracelets. Well, she didn't quite *make* them. Her uncle arranged to have them shipped in from Indonesia. Angela claimed to have designed them, but I had my doubts. She probably picked them out of some *Illegal Sweatshops 'R Us* catalog. I suspected that part of the reason she'd pushed Chris so hard to cast me was because she wanted to find an excuse to get her jewelry on TV. As a family member of a station employee, she wasn't allowed to be a Wife. Over the years we had stayed in touch sporadically. Since I'd joined the show, I'd seen her at least three times a week. Interesting, right? But, perhaps I was being cynical.

"Okay, great. Help yourself to some coffee. I'll be down in a few."

After I showered and put on my trusty Clinique foundation, my skin looked somewhat normal. I squeezed into a faded pair of jeans and joined Angela in the kitchen. My sister Deirdre and my father stood at the center island, organizing the ingredients for the brownies. Angela arranged her owls on the kitchen table. Deirdre, eighteen months my junior, was a Special Ed teacher married to her college sweetheart, the dishy Gordon Pederson. She wasn't too happy about appearing on the show. Deirdre said she didn't want to piss off her school board, but I suspected that there was a little bit of younger sister jealousy going on there. But Dee had agreed once I told her she could mention the reading flashcards she'd developed and hoped to sell on her new website. The new website, by the way, which my dear sister had blackmailed me into financing out of my *Gold Coast Wives* stipend.

Angela looked up from her owls. "Oh, sweetie, you look much better. You had me worried."

"Worried?" Deirdre asked.

I poured myself a cup of coffee. "Nothing, it's a long story. Are you really going to wear that thing?"

"It's an apron, Kate," Dee snapped. "We're supposed to be cooking, remember? I have aprons for you and Mom, and I made little ones for the kids. Sorry, Ang, I didn't know you'd be here, so I don't have one for you."

"It's an apron with *Miss Dee's Phonics Fun* written all over it," I said. "Along with a website address."

"So?"

"So it's not very subtle, Dee. I thought we'd agreed we'd mention your flash cards in conversation, naturally. I didn't think we'd put up billboards all over my kitchen."

"They're not billboards, they're aprons and totally appropriate for today's taping. Don't you agree, Angela?"

"Oh don't ask her. Angela and her frickin' owls. She'd make Dad put on the owls if she could."

"I'm coming out with a men's line. I can bring some pieces next time, Mr. Griffin, if you'd like," Angela offered.

"I think that's my cue to leave. Ladies, enjoy your brownies. And your owls." My father escaped to Bill O'Reilly in the den.

"Smart man," I said. "Okay girls, I don't mind you if you plug your products. Hell, everyone else on the show is doing it. But, let's just try and be a little bit classy about it."

"Of course. When am I not classy?" Angela asked.

Not wanting to go there, I said, "Well, let's be subtle. Do you hear me, Dee? Subtle."

"Oh, relax," Deirdre said as she measured the flour.

Looked like we were making these bad boys from scratch. Isn't it easier to just use Betty Crocker?

"How was last night? What are the other Wives like?" Deirdre asked.

"Why don't you tell her, Angela?"

"What do you mean?"

"Why don't you tell her about the other Wives?"

Angela busied herself by untangling an owl's gold chain. "You're the one on the show."

"First, there's Rachel Finley who owns Finley's Fine Furnishings. She's a little too Queens for my taste, but she's nice enough. Plus, she'll probably give me a discount if I'm ever flush enough to buy furniture again. Then there's Tina Andrews--Camilla Yardley from *Hope's Glen*--who seems somewhat kooky, but harmless enough. And finally, there's Pamela Kruger."

"Who's Pamela Kruger?"

"Angela, tell her who Pamela Kruger is."

"Oh, for Chrissake," Angela sniped. "It's Pamela Reynolds."

"Pamela Reynolds from Queen of the Rosary Academy? That Pamela Reynolds?" my sister asked.

"Yes, *that* Pamela Reynolds. And of course, she totally pretended not to recognize me. She even called me Kathy Griffin and asked if I was a comedienne, if you can believe it."

"Maybe she really didn't recognize you. High school was a long time ago. Plus you used to be less, well, less large," Angela said.

"She broke my ankle!" I shouted. "I'd think you'd remember breaking someone's bones."

"Oh, it was like a million years ago," Angela said. "It was an accident, let it go."

"It would've been nice to have a little warning, that's all. Did you tell Chris about our high school rivalry? Is that why we're both on the show?"

"Rivalry? Are you kidding me? You and Pamela didn't have any kind of rivalry. I also don't remember her being so bad. In fact she was kind of fun. She threw a fantastic Sweet Sixteen party."

"Yeah, which I wasn't invited to."

"You're being pissy because Pamela Reynolds didn't invite you to a birthday party?"

"You know what, Angela, just forget it. You were one of the *beautiful people* in high school. You have no idea what it was like for the rest of us."

"Please, Kate, don't go all *Pretty in Pink* on me."

"How did she look?" Deirdre asked, in what I think was an attempt to change the subject.

"Amazing," I admitted. "Older of course, but if anything she's improved, become more elegant. Boobs a little bigger, but they look real. No lines on her face, but she looks natural, not like she's used Botox. I do think she might have had some collagen shots in her lips. She looks, I don't know, glossy--like those society women shopping on Madison Avenue look glossy."

"Girls, are you aware the cameras are on?" my mother asked as she entered the kitchen holding three hardcopies of her most recent romances from Heartland Press.

Shit.

"Oh, Mom," Deirdre said as she looked straight into the camera above the microwave, "are those your latest novels? Thanks so much for bringing them. The teachers at my school are always asking for autographed copies."

"That's not a problem, darling," my mother said in a strange Queen Elizabeth accent. "Nothing's too much trouble for my fans."

"People are always impressed that my mother, Grace Griffin, is the real Penelope La Montagne!" Deirdre said with a flourish. Okay, I was going to be a little sick.

"Oh, my darling," Grace said, "you're embarrassing me." Again with *darling*?

"Why should you be embarrassed? Writing twenty Heartland romance novels is such an accomplishment!"

"Actually, my dear, it will soon be twenty one. I'm putting the finishing touches on my latest novel, *A Pocketful of Gold*."

"Mrs. Griffin, I just can't wait to read it!" Angela gushed. She was getting in on the action too?

"It will be published soon, and I'll be sure to give a copy to both you and your mother. I love the fact that young, stylish women like you in the twenty five to forty-five-year-old demographic enjoy reading the Penelope La Montagne books as much as your mothers do."

"We do, Mrs. Griffin."

"Angela, what a beautiful necklace you have on," my mother simpered.

This was getting to be too much. "Aren't we supposed to be making brownies or something?" I asked.

Ignoring me, Angela said, "Didn't Kate mention my new jewelry line? Angela Rosetti Fine Jewelry has a complete line of earrings, necklaces, bracelets and rings. I'm even starting a men's collection!"

"These are beautiful. I hope Mr. Griffin buys me one of these beautiful owl necklaces for Christmas." My mother had never worn any jewelry other than her plain gold wedding band. Last Christmas my father had bought her a printer.

"He won't have to…as a special gift, I'm giving the three of you ladies the owl pendent of your choice!"

"Oh, I'll take the kissing owls please," Deirdre said. "They're so unusual. I know all the teachers at school will want one. Where can they buy them?"

"My jewelry line is only available on my website, AngelasOwls.com. I accept MasterCard, Visa and Pay Pal."

"Deirdre, don't you think we should start on those brownies?" I asked.

"Yes, but first you have to put on your aprons."

And, of course it went downhill from there. As my three-year-old daughter Lucy and my niece and nephew spread brownie frosting all over their faces and my speckled granite, Deirdre talked about her flash cards, Angela about her owls, and Mom went into excruciating detail about Fiona, Lord Cartwright and their love triangle--which probably wasn't the best topic in front of the children. At one point I left the room and joined my father and Greta Van Susteren in the den. Eventually the brownies were made, the products plugged and the two hour taping session thankfully came to an end.

"I think that went well. My new editor at Heartland will surely be impressed," my mother said with forced enthusiasm as she put on the kettle for a pot of tea. My mother's new editor had recently made noises about not renewing her contract if sales didn't improve. My mother had implied she might be ready to retire her writing alter ego. She wasn't fooling anybody. We all knew she was gutted by the threat of losing her second lusty life as Penelope La Montagne.

"I hope I get some orders for the flash cards, although I still have to figure out how to make them." Deirdre wrapped the brownies in Saran Wrap.

"My Uncle Frank can help you with that. His company is making my jewelry. He's coming over to my house for dinner on Sunday. Why don't you and your husband join us?"

"Oh, Angela, do you think he can help?"

"Of course, Dee, don't worry about a thing. Kate, this has been fun, but I really gotta go." Angela handed me a large jewelry case. "Here, this is a complete collection of the owls. Chrissy told me you didn't wear them yesterday, which, given the circumstances, may be just as well. Could you wear at least one owl piece to Pamela's luncheon?"

"What luncheon?" I grabbed the taping schedule. I couldn't believe I had forgotten another event.

"Her luncheon on Thursday? Tom sent out a revised schedule this morning. Check your email."

I flipped open my laptop. I saw a few messages from NYJimmy66, my missing husband's catchy new email address, which I'd have to read later, and one from someone trying to enlarge my penis. But none from Tom or anyone at Channel 45.

"Do you think I'm not invited?"

"Oh, please, Kate. Tom probably forgot to send you an email. I'm sure you're invited. It's a LICKs Ball planning session. Even I'm going, since I'm donating my entire owl collection as a silent auction item."

Dee giggled. "What's a LICKs Ball? That can't be the name."

I got it.

Angela rolled her eyes. "I know, like, hasn't anyone told her?"

"I'm not about to. I've already alienated one Wife, I have to keep the others on my side," I said.

"Okay, I've got to fly." Angela flung her oversize Birkin bag over her shoulder. "I'll see you on Thursday, sweetie."

"If I'm even invited."

"Oh, Molly Ringwald, I'm sure you're invited. Bye bye," she trilled.

After Angela left, I called Tom's cellphone and he told me, sounding somewhat ashamed, I was not invited to Pamela's luncheon. Apparently, Pamela was concerned about her furniture, given my reign of destruction at the cocktail party. Instead, production scheduled a one-on-one lunch with me and Rachel at my house for later in the week.

Deirdre rubbed my shoulder. "Come on, don't be upset. You can't let someone like Pamela get to you."

"I know," I said with a sigh. "You know what, guys, I think I'll go lie down. These Benadryl are making me tired. You don't mind if I skip dinner at your house, Dee, do you?"

"Not at all. We'll take Lucy with us, so you can rest."

After a two hour nap in a quiet house, I felt like a new woman. A new woman who didn't care about Pamela and her revoked invitations. A new woman who was ready to read her missing husband's emails. With a pot of tea and several brownies to fortify me, I opened my email account.

Kate,

Do you really think by threatening to sell my car you're going to make me come home? I'm on a journey here. I cannot believe that you are so selfish that you would try and ruin that for me. I'll come home when I'm good and ready.

Jim

After months of placating him via email, tiptoeing around his fragile ego, hell, even acting interested in his explanation of the migratory habits of the kangaroo, I'd finally had enough. I hit the reply button and typed:

Fine, then don't come home.

I was going to need something a little stronger than tea.

* * * *

On Wednesday morning, running late of course, Lucy and I jumped into the beautiful silver BMW X3 I'd probably need to sell at some point--hello, Kia--and made it to her Ballet for Tots class ten minutes late. I changed Lucy's shoes and led her into class. I flopped onto one of the folding chairs that lined the hall outside the classroom and tried to distract myself with *The New York Times*.

As I scanned the Metro section, I could hear the murmur of the other moms clustered down the hall. I looked up and could see, to my dismay, that the eight women were at least ten years younger than me and fell into the category of *yummy mummies*. Deirdre had once described the typical Long Island type: thin from her many yoga and pilates classes, perfectly plucked, highlighted and waxed from her many salon treatments--after all, she deserved some *me* time--generally outfitted in *casual* wear that cost more than Deirdre's monthly mortgage, slightly over-caffeinated from her Starbucks addiction, who spoke in the high, nasal voice of the true *Lawn Guylander*. Given my prior work schedule and the fact that we'd recently moved back to Long Island, I'd had limited contact with the other Island mommies. Marion, Lucy's last nanny, had ferried Lucy to her various dance and music classes. So, the only mommies I'd met were the other working mothers who hit the playgrounds on the weekends. And we'd all been so exhausted, we didn't have the energy to be either competitive or friendly.

I mentally compared my size fourteen Gap jeans and sweatshirt to the skintight Juicy Couture ensemble sported by the blond twenty-something mom clutching a venti latte to my right. It had to have taken her at least thirty minutes to achieve such pin-straight locks. It had taken me exactly two minutes to pull my gnarled red curls up in a scrunchie. Why on earth would someone get dolled up to sit in the corridor of a YMCA?

I glanced at the group and caught a dark-haired fashionista looking me up and down. God, this was worse than the high school cafeteria. Except in high school I'd only worried about acne and ten extra pounds. Now I had to contend with forty extra pounds, frumpy clothes and no husband. Although I was feeling quite sorry for myself, I gave Miss Vogue what I hoped was a confident, detached smile before trying to concentrate on my newspaper. After class, I was helping Lucy change her shoes when a tall woman around thirty came up to me. "Is Marion okay? She's not sick or anything, is she?"

I forced a smile. "Oh no, she's fine. My work schedule has changed, so I'll be taking Lucy to dance class from now on. My name is Kate Ryan, by the way." I offered my hand.

"I'm Melissa Green, Stephanie's mom. I just love Marion. Do you know if she'll be coming to Bunco on Thursday? It's at my house this week." Marion played Bunco with these people?

"I don't know. Do you want me to call and ask?"

"That's okay, I have her number. Bye now." And with that, she and little Stephanie hurried down the hallway.

Was there a secret password I was missing?

I zippered Lucy's pink Cinderella parka and walked out of the Y. I couldn't believe I had to come back in two days. I'd have to hit the mall before then. Aside from the few outfits I bought for the show, my wardrobe at the moment consisted of expensive suits, an assortment of silk blouses and several pairs of subdued pumps--perfect for a Park Avenue attorney, not so great for an unemployed suburban mom.

I further pondered my wardrobe conundrum and financial destitution while I drove Lucy to Sundays, an old fashioned luncheonette in Huntington village. I knew I shouldn't have wasted money on meals out, but Lucy was a fairly picky eater, and I didn't always have the energy to fight with her. Lucky for me, even she couldn't resist their challah bread French toast. As I headed for an open booth in the back, I noticed the place was overrun with yummy mummies and their spawn. There wasn't one mother eating with her child--they were in groups of three or more mommies. I quickly grabbed Lucy's hand and ran for the door.

Was I really so pathetic that I couldn't eat with my child in a public place without feeling insecure? Did I really once form billion dollar hedge funds and advise titans on Wall Street?

At home I made Lucy a sad approximation of Sundays' French toast which, surprise, surprise, she didn't eat. I then cleaned the house until it sparkled, confirmed that Elaine had ordered a sumptuous spread from Cora's Concepts in Catering, and managed to convince my parents to go shopping for kitchen cabinets and take Lucy with them. Rachel and the *Gold Coast Wives* crew were due at my house that afternoon. There was nothing that could go wrong for this taping. I needed to prove to myself, and to Channel 45, I was not a complete loser Wife.

I dressed in a long, black wool skirt paired with a dark green merino sweater and black ballet flats. I also wore a long silver owl necklace, which would hopefully placate Angela. The crew arrived at noon to set up, and Rachel arrived at one on the dot.

"What a stunning home," Rachel said as I opened the front door. "I can't wait to see the inside!"

"We moved in recently so there's not much to see, but please come in."

"I love what you've done with this hallway. That brass mirror is stunning."

I smiled. "Jim and I picked it up at an antique shop we came across in Maine one summer, before we'd even bought a house."

"What a find! You have a good eye."

"I'm pretty hopeless when it comes to decorating or fashion, to tell you the truth. My husband picked it out."

We entered the formal living room. "And this room is from last year's Ethan Allen catalogue, am I right?"

I laughed. "Jim was really busy last year, and I was sick of staring at yet another empty room, so I let the saleswoman go to town. Do you think it's awful?"

"Not awful, a bit generic though. I think if you added some interesting accent pieces, you could break it up," Rachel said. Wow, she wasn't just a whiny cat fancier from Queens--she seemed to really know her stuff.

"Sad to say, this is the best room in the house. The rest of the rooms are either empty or furnished with pieces from our apartment in the city--some of them look like doll furniture."

"I see what you mean, but I love this great room. The light is amazing and that stone fireplace is to die for. This room has so many possibilities. When you have a two-story room and ceilings of this height, you need to be careful with the decor and the dimensions. You don't want people to feel like they're in an airplane hangar."

"This room is definitely next on our priority list." If the bank didn't repossess the house first, I thought. I led her to the kitchen. "I hope you're hungry because Elaine ordered enough food for an army."

"No carbs, I hope. I'm not doing carbs now." Rachel couldn't weigh more than a hundred pounds.

"I think I have a little bit of everything."

Rachel nibbled on a few slices of chicken breast while she filled me in on the charity ball developments. Given it was less than five weeks away, most of the work had been done. I agreed to help set up before the event, and I committed to buy a table. Seemed easy enough.

"Kate, I have a wonderful idea. How would you feel about Finley's Fine Furnishings decorating your great room?"

"That would be...great."

"Perfect. I'll have my designer Garrett come take measurements tomorrow."

"Tomorrow? I wasn't planning on buying any new furniture this year."

"You don't want my help?" she asked, looking very offended.

"Of course I do, it's just I hadn't budgeted for new furniture this year. It's not the best time for me to be making big expenditures," I said, a bit annoyed. I really didn't want to discuss the state of my finances on air.

"Let me talk to David. If you would allow us to film the design process on the show and include before and after shots on our website and print ads, I could do it for you at cost."

"Rachel, that is so generous of you. It's not that I'm not grateful, because I am. Very grateful. However, I've suffered some financial setbacks, and since I'm not working right now, I can't afford to make any large purchases." I couldn't believe I had to say this on camera.

"Oh," Rachel said, surprised. "I had no idea things were so bad for you. I thought you said you were taking time off to spend with your daughter."

"I am enjoying spending time with my daughter, but it's more complicated than that."

Rachel patted my hand. "Not to worry, sweetheart. Let me talk to David and see what we can do."

"Really, it's fine. I've been staring at the empty great room for close to two years. A few more months won't kill me."

"Leave it to me." Rachel was a woman with a mission. Well, whatever. I had enough things to worry about and the great room was last on my list.

After Rachel left I checked my emails, and there were no more missives from NYJimmy66. Disappointing but not unexpected. There was an invitation to the New York Asset Managers Symposium in April where I'd taught a seminar the previous year. I decided to sign up. It might be a good networking opportunity, and at the very least I would earn some much needed continuing legal education credits. I might not be practicing law any longer, but I didn't want to lose my license either.

With that taken care of, I loaded the dishwasher and vacuumed the kitchen. I had gone to law school so I wouldn't have to vacuum. Unfortunately, my austerity budget no longer covered weekly visits from the Miracle Maids. Lucy found it funny that I was doing housework-- she treated it like a little game and jumped over the vacuum hose. As I finished vacuuming, the phone rang.

"Kathleen, thank God you're there," whined my mother-in-law. "I haven't been able to get in touch with you, and I was afraid something was wrong."

Oh shit. I'd have to start checking my caller ID. I took a deep breath. "We're fine, Peg," I said, trying not to let my irritation be too obvious to my mother-in-law.

"Have you heard from Jim? He's stopped answering my emails, some guilt trip nonsense."

"I received a similar email about two weeks ago."

"What do you plan to do?" demanded Peg.

"What would you like me to do?"

"Go find him. Bring him home."

"How do you suggest I do that? I don't even know where he is exactly. Australia's a big place you know."

"It sounds to me like you don't even care whether he comes home or not," she huffed. Of course Jim's mother would make this all my fault.

"I'm not the one who left, Peg. Right now I'm focusing on taking care of my daughter and not losing my home," I said with what I hoped was a patient tone. I'd learned from experience it didn't pay to antagonize Peg.

"Losing your home? Oh don't be so dramatic."

"I'm sorry, but I was on my way out. Is there something else?"

"I have a stack of bills here that I can make neither heads nor tails of. And there are second notices coming. You know how Jimmy usually handles my bills. And the furnace is making some funny noises."

"Have you called Linda? She's an accountant. She could help you with the bills."

"It's tax time, and she's run off her feet."

"What about Maura?" I suggested. "She doesn't work."

"I couldn't trust Maura with something like this."

"You couldn't trust Maura with writing a few checks and calling a repairman?" I asked, exasperated.

"Now, Kathleen, you need to come out and help me with this. It was Jimmy's job and since he's no longer here, you must help me."

"Is this a joke? Are you kidding me?" I said, my voice getting louder.

"Of course I'm not kidding."

"I absolutely will *not* help you. You have four daughters at your disposal. It's not my fault your children run from you like the plague. Here's a thought, Peg, why not try doing these things yourself? You're not an invalid."

"I cannot believe you are speaking to me this way."

"Well, believe it." I slammed down the phone.

After a few deep breaths I continued my cleaning frenzy. I'd never realized what a stress reliever cleaning could be. Those cleaning ladies might not have had it so bad after all. I was tidying up the playroom when my parents came back. After a pot of tea and a discussion of the pros and cons of laminate versus wood cabinets, my father decided to drive to their house in Massapequa and take some measurements. My father's a real homebody, and I thought living in my house, especially amidst the *Gold Coast Wives* nonsense, was a strain on him.

With a sigh, my mother opened her laptop. Writing usually energized her, but she didn't seem like herself either.

"Mom, what's wrong? Do you miss your house?"

"No. I've actually enjoyed staying here. It makes me feel a bit like a movie star. No, I'm having trouble with my ending. Truth be told, I'm having trouble with the whole novel. It's just not flowing the way my other books did."

"Maybe the pressure Heartland is putting on you is too much."

"That probably doesn't help, but I think it might be time for me to retire, hang it up." This defeated woman wasn't the Grace Griffin I knew.

"You still love writing, don't you?"

"I do, but I can't seem to write the type of romances readers want nowadays."

"Have you ever tried writing something else? What about a memoir or fiction based on your own experiences?"

"Oh," scoffed my mother, "who would want to read about a suburban housewife?"

"Plenty of people. If you don't want to write about your married years, what about your childhood or your family back in Limerick? Maybe write a book about a girl who decides to leave her home and immigrate to a faraway land."

"Maybe you should be the writer," Mom said. "You make my life sound so exciting and unique."

"Mom, it was exciting and unique. Dee and I loved hearing your stories about the farm and how you used to steal your brother's bicycle to sneak down to the dances held at the crossroad. There's plenty you could write about."

"Would Americans want to read things like that? I don't know."

"Memoirs from Irish writers are all the rage, Mom. What about the one you gave me last Christmas?"

"Oh for God's sake, I would never write a book like that. Shaming your family and airing your dirty laundry for the whole world to see."

"When you put it that way, it sounds a bit like what I'm doing with *Gold Coast Wives*."

"But my life wasn't anything like that fella's," my mother continued, ignoring me. "My father had one of the finest farms in three counties. We weren't living in a slum, and my father wasn't drinking the rent money."

"I didn't say you were anything like that, Mom. All I'm saying is you had a unique experience. With your writing skills, people might find your life story interesting. If you're not comfortable 'airing your dirty laundry,' then fictionalize your experience."

"I don't know. I still have to finish *A Pocketful of Gold.*"

"Turn it in as is. They're probably going to cancel your contract anyway," I said.

"Maybe."

"Mom, if Jim's leaving me--and I'm finally admitting it now, he's left me--if that's taught me anything, it's that sometimes being the good girl and doing the right thing doesn't always pay off. Look at me, I bore his child and for over ten years made his dinner and cleaned his house--or at least supervised. And what did it get me? On my own at forty two. I'm getting a little off track here. What I meant to say is, don't write what Heartland wants or what you think the family would approve of. Write what *you* want, what makes you happy."

She stared at me for a moment. "Girl, you're right. Hand me that laptop. I'm going to email my book to Heartland right now before I lose my nerve. Let the chips fall where they may."

"That's the spirit!"

"And once you're done with this reality show mess, maybe you should take some of your own advice. Find what makes you happy. Move on from Jim. Any man who leaves a good woman is a fool and not worth crying over. You're a good woman, Kate."

"Thank you, Mom."

"And another thing," Grace said. "Don't let this house be an albatross around your neck. At the end of the day, it's only four walls. Sell it, cut your losses and buy something more manageable."

"I know you're right. But I thought if I could keep everything together, Jim would eventually come to his senses, I'd find a job and everything would go back to the way it was."

My mother took my hand. "I know you did, Katie, but would you really want it to? Could you welcome him home with open arms after everything he's put you through?"

"I don't know. Maybe."

"I know it's a hard fact to face, but it's been months now. You have to assume he's not coming home and to start living your life. I know you don't believe this, but you're still a young woman, still an attractive woman."

"Too bad this isn't on tape. Channel 45 would probably give us our own advice show."

"Hey do you hear something?" she asked, looking around the kitchen.

"It's the dishwasher I think." I looked at my watch. "It's almost three. I'd better pick up Lucy."

"Right. And I'd better start on my new book. My writing group is going to be surprised."

"They're going to love it, Mom. I know they will."

"You know what? I don't care whether they do or not. I'm writing this book for me."

Chapter 2

Next morning, bright and early, a short, sprite-like man, followed by a Channel 45 crew, rang my doorbell.

"Kate Ryan? Hello! I'm Garrett Bliss from Finley's Fine Furnishings! I'm here to take measurements!" He was a little too peppy for eight in the morning.

"I don't understand," I mumbled, closing Jim's old bathrobe.

"Rachel will call you later to go over the details. Can I come in? My day is pretty booked, and I squeezed you in as it is."

"Sure, come on in." This train seemed to have left the station, so I might as well jump on.

Garrett and the crew, including assistant director Tom and his nose ring, barreled in and set up their equipment in the great room. While they were busy, I got dressed--fat mommy jeans to the rescue--and ran Lucy to nursery school. On my way home I picked up an order of bagels, a dozen donuts and a box of Dunkin' Donuts coffee for the crew. Maybe if I bribed them with carbs and sugar, the camera men would film me on my good side, or at least limit the number of ass shots.

"Bagels and donuts, ooh you're bad," Garrett trilled after I laid out my little feast.

"Help yourself."

Garrett grabbed half a bagel. How decadent.

"Kate, what is your vision for this room?"

"Vision?" Not empty. Did that constitute a vision? "I don't know, traditional?"

"I'm thinking French country. French country with a twist."

"As long as it's kid friendly, I don't mind." I stuffed a Boston creme donut in my mouth.

"We can do that. Rachel wants this done by the weekend, so we're limited to items in stock. It's a challenge, but I'm up for it!" He looked like he'd won the lottery. How could fabric make someone so happy? I'd never get it.

"That's only two days away."

"It's going to be fantastic. You just have to trust me."

"I'm sure you'll do a wonderful job, Garrett. Certainly better than anything I would do."

"I'll do my best," he said modestly.

"Only make sure it's durable, especially the couch. My Lucy is a bit of a terror."

"Understood. Could you and your daughter possibly stay somewhere else for two days? There'll be a lot of dust and paint, plus Rachel and the producers would like to film this to be a surprise."

"Oh, like that show on TV? Does that mean I have to cry?" I joked. When Garrett didn't crack a smile I said in a more serious tone, "Only kidding. Not a problem, we're supposed to film my 'at home' segments this week. I'll just call Elaine and ask her what she wants us to do."

After a bagel and another donut, I called Elaine and she confirmed I would not be responsible for the cost of the great room redecoration. It would be split between Channel 45 and Finley's. I think she was a bit put out that I wasn't more grateful, but really, there's only so much enthusiasm I could work up for a free couch.

Elaine and I discussed this week's tapings and agreed to move the *at home* tapings to Dee's house. My sister would be thrilled for another opportunity to discuss the wonders of Miss Dee's Phonics Fun. After I hung up with Elaine, I walked to the guest room to tell my parents the change in plans, but my mother was already packing.

"Oh, did Tom tell you about the move?"

"What move?" my mother asked as she folded one of her many pairs of black pants.

"We need to make ourselves scarce because of the work on the great room."

"Oh, I didn't know. Your father and I decided it was time for us to move home. I can't work on my new book here with all these distractions."

"What about the fire damage?" I asked, trying not to smile.

"Your father and Uncle Danny went over at the house yesterday, and everything's fine now. I hope you're not upset that we're leaving." Mom stuffed an extra pair of shoes into her overflowing case.

"Well, we will miss you," I said, which was true. I had gotten used to living with my parents again, used to feeling loved, protected and aggravated all at the same time. I had even gotten used to Bill O'Reilly. "But don't worry, I understand. When your muse calls, you must answer."

"Exactly!"

I helped my mother pack the rest of their things, and my father carried the bags to their red Chevy. "Sweetheart," my father said, giving me his signature peck on the cheek, "thanks for puttin' up with us."

"No, Dad, thank you for all your help with Lucy. She'll miss you."

"She's a smart cookie, just like her mother. Now take care of yourself, and don't let those crazy TV people push you around."

"I'll try not to."

"Enough already, Johnny," my mother shouted from the front seat, "you'll see her next week."

My father squeezed my shoulder and then folded all six feet, three inches of himself into the compact.

My parents had barely made it out the driveway before Tom met me at the front door. "Call Harry immediately." Harry was the show's director.

Geez, what could be such an emergency? These people would never last long at Fowler Sherman. "Fine, Tom, I'll call him now."

"Hi, Harry," I said into the phone, "what's up?"

"There's been a change in the schedule. We need to add you to one more group event this Saturday."

"That's short notice, Harry. I have my uncle's surprise sixtieth birthday party this Saturday."

"Sorry, but we need you."

"What's the event? Why am I only hearing about it now?"

"It's a launch party for Pamela's new book. Tina had to pull out."

"Oh, so you were going to have an event for Pamela and not invite me again? And now you want me drop everything and come running?"

"It's not exactly like that. The book launch was only finalized last week." Harry sounded embarrassed.

"It still doesn't explain why you're only telling me now. My answer is no." I hung up and stomped into the house.

Ten minutes later, Elaine called. "Kate," she said in a cold tone, "what's this I hear about you not attending Pamela's book launch?"

"I have other plans, sorry."

"According to your contract, you're obligated to participate in group events."

I grabbed a copy of the contract from the desk drawer and quickly flipped through it. "If you read Schedule One you'll see that I'm contractually obligated to participate in only three group events: the cocktail party, the spa day and the charity ball. A book launch party is not listed anywhere in my contract." My friend Glenn Meyers, an entertainment law expert, had added all kinds of protective provisions as riders to Channel 45's standard contract. Thank you, Glenn Meyers.

"It can't possibly say that. That's not our standard contract."

"I can have my attorney email you a copy if you'd like."

"Kate, please," she said in a more wheedling tone, "can't you do me this favor?"

"This favor for Pamela you mean, and no I cannot."

"If I don't have at least three Wives at this event, it will screw with my budget. Please, what can I do to make you say yes?"

Power. I liked this. "Perhaps I could swing by for an hour before my uncle's party."

"Wonderful!"

"I don't have a thing to wear."

"Not a problem," Elaine said. "I'll send Chris over with a dress--something nice, something expensive."

"And matching non-owl jewelry?"

"Yes, I'll see what I can do."

"Also, I didn't receive an invitation."

"We'll messenger one over this afternoon."

"I think I'd like a personal invitation," I said. "From the author."

"What do you mean?"

"I'd like Pamela to be here within the hour. And since Tom is already here, I'd like the invitation taped."

"I don't know if she's available," Elaine said without conviction.

"Tell her to make herself available, or I'll be a no-show."

"Okay," Elaine said in defeat. "I'll track her down."

"Good. Also, I want her to admit on tape that we did go to high school together, that we did graduate the same year and to apologize for pretending not to know me."

"Kate, is this really necessary? Aren't you being a little childish?"

"I don't care. Tell her to be here in an hour, or I'm leaving." Man, this felt great. Maybe I'd hijack a plane next.

I quickly changed into one of the elegant matron outfits Chris had selected, hid the donut boxes and made a fresh pot of coffee. Thirty minutes later, the doorbell rang. The camera men jumped into position. I plastered a fake smile on my face and opened the door.

"Pamela, what a surprise!" Pamela stood on my front steps working the edgy look by wearing large oversize sunglasses--*hello*, it's March--a tight black leather jacket and dark flared jeans. I looked like a prosperous librarian. It was impossible not to hate this woman.

"Hello, Kate. I hope you don't mind me dropping by unannounced," Pamela said, not missing a beat. "I realized I never gave you an invitation to my book launch. I do apologize for the oversight." She handed me a large gold envelope.

"A book launch!" I practically shouted with glee. "Why don't you come in for a cup of coffee and tell me all about it?"

"I'd love to," Pamela cooed. "I can only stay a few minutes. I have a meeting with my publicist."

"I didn't know you were a writer," I said as we entered the kitchen.

"I've loved writing ever since I was a teenager. Perhaps you remember some of the articles I wrote for the school newspaper?"

"I don't remember them, no." I pretended to think very hard. I didn't remember them because there weren't any. Miss Homecoming Queen wouldn't have stepped within ten feet of the dank basement-level newspaper office staffed with English honors geeks like me.

"Well, that's understandable. High school was a long time ago. I suppose that's why I didn't recognize you at first. After the cocktail party I flipped through my old yearbook and realized I *did* know you. I think we even cheered on the same cheerleading team, didn't we? Anyway, I apologize if I made you feel uncomfortable in any way." Wow, she was good.

"Not at all. Think nothing of it." Yeah, think nothing of breaking my ankle.

"Because, you know, Kate, I pride myself in making people feel comfortable when I'm entertaining. It's a passion of mine. That's why I was inspired to write my book, *Gold Coast Entertaining.*"

"Snappy title."

"Oh, do you like it?"

"Oh, I do!"

"I'm so glad you can come to my book launch," Pamela said with equal enthusiasm. "Don will be pleased. He really enjoyed chatting with you the other night about business and such."

"I'm looking forward to it. Can I get you more coffee?"

"No thank you, I have to go." Pamela leaned in and gave me a kiss that didn't come within six inches of my cheek. "See you Saturday." And she scooted out the door.

Tom and some of the other camera men tried hard not to laugh as I walked over to the door and gave her a big wave. Maybe I should've considered acting as my new career.

* * * *

I was black and blue after two days of sleeping on the torture device Deirdre calls a pull-out couch. However, the two days weren't a total loss since Harry and crew finished all of my *at home* tapings. They filmed us bathing the kids, baking cookies and even devoted a two-hour taping session exclusively to my sister's husband Gordon, looking very delicious in a too tight Phonics Fun t-shirt, as he gave the kids a soccer lesson. It's possible one of the camera men might have had a crush on Gordon. That done, I only had to make it through the great room reveal, Pamela's book launch, the spa day and the LICKs Ball, and I could hang it up as a Gold Coast Wife for good. Thank God.

Tom instructed me to be back at my house by eleven Saturday morning. Since Deirdre didn't want to use up another sick day staying home and playing with us, Lucy and I left my sister's tidy split-level on the South Shore at nine and drove to Sundays. Lucy and I enjoyed a leisurely breakfast of challah bread French toast and sausage links. I was on my second cup of coffee when two of the dance class yummy mummies came in with several children toddling behind them. Both gave me big smiles and one even said, "Hi Kate!" Wow. Who knew, I might score a Bunco invite yet.

Rachel, Garrett, Tom and the camera crew were already at the house when I pulled up at ten to eleven. I opened the front door to Rachel barking orders at Garrett.

"Kate, sweetheart," Rachel said mid-rant, "we're putting on the finishing touches. Would you mind waiting in the kitchen until we're ready?"

"Not a problem. Would anyone like some coffee?"

"Oh, you are a doll! I would love a cup," Rachel said as she tottered back to the great room in her four-inch heels.

I busied myself with the coffee. Lucy peeked into the great room. "Oh, Mommy," she said running into the kitchen. "It's beautiful and shiny!"

Shiny? Is French country supposed to be shiny?

"All right, Kate," Garrett announced with a camera man behind him. "We're ready. Are you excited?"

"Sure." Garrett looked a little deflated by my lack of enthusiasm, so I tried a bit harder. "I'm so excited."

"I know you're going to love it!" Garrett said. I hoped for his sake I did. I thought disappointing Garrett would be like smacking a puppy.

Lucy ran ahead of me. I entered the great room.

"Is this fabulous, or what!" Rachel exclaimed.

Fabulous?

"And it's sophisticated, Kate. Sophisticated with a twist," Garrett added.

Sophisticated? I may not know much about design, but I wouldn't have used fabulous or sophisticated to describe the decor. More like loud, garish, or maybe...horrible?

The walls were painted a soft blue that I loved, and the couches and two arm chairs were made of a soft buttery yellow material that was nice--I guessed this was where the French country came in. However, they were covered with so many aquamarine satin throw pillows and blankets that it wasn't clear how one was supposed to sit on them. In fact, Lucy used a pillow to slide off the couch, which she thought was great fun. Glass and crystal figurines covered every available surface and a huge armoire-type cabinet made of mirrors housed a further assortment of figurines. The effect was blinding. Parts of the walls were covered with what I thought were tapestries in shades of neon blue.

"It's very colorful," I said. A true statement.

"I know, doesn't it just liven up the house?" Rachel said. "No offense, Kate, but your house was really drab before."

"What else do you love?" Garrett asked.

The camera man zoomed in on me as I said, "The couches?" Yet another true statement.

Rachel hit Garrett on the arm. "See, I knew she'd love the couches."

"What else?"

I was running out of true statements. "The lamps?" Their bases were nice. The crystal encrusted shades I could do without.

"And this is all yours to keep, Kate. Except the piano--it'll have to go back this afternoon." Given it was a piano that would make Liberace proud, no great loss there.

Looking into the camera, Rachel continued, "David and I are proud that we were able to help a neighbor in need. It's not easy being an unemployed single mother and, Kate, we're grateful we could make the very hard road that you're traveling a little easier." With crystal figurines? "This is what Finley's Fine Furnishings is all about. Giving back to our community!"

I would have really loved to tell Rachel what she could do with her crystal animals and her community, but what good would that have done? Better to just smile and get her out of here as soon as possible. "Thank you, Rachel and Garrett, for all of your hard work." Garrett beamed.

"You are more than welcome, sweetie. Now, give momma a hug!" Rachel's stick-like limbs surrounded my torso.

The taping session was finally over. Rachel said she'd be back in an hour with the photographer for the print ads. Garrett was going to stay and put more *finishing touches* on the room. What more could he possibly add--a waterfall? Garrett agreed to keep an eye on Lucy while I went upstairs to take a much needed bath. The strain of pretending to like crystal panthers--yes, there was a whole family of crystal feline animals--had given me a headache.

A bubble bath and a trashy magazine, what could be better? Poor Jennifer Aniston and her search for love. I felt like giving her a call and telling her to hit the local sperm bank instead. Then again, perhaps I was a little bitter and not in the best position to advise Jennifer. I was just getting caught up on Lindsay Lohan's latest antics when I heard the crash.

"Oh, nooo," Garrett wailed.

I jumped out of the bath, threw on Jim's old bathrobe and ran down the stairs.

Garrett sobbed as he picked up shards of the panther figurine. Lucy cowered in the corner.

"Mommy, I only wanted to play with the cats. I wasn't trying to hurt them."

"I know, sweetie, I know. Why don't you go into the den, and I'll put on some Dora?" I turned to Garrett, "Are you okay?"

"She's going to kill me," Garrett whispered.

"Don't worry about a thing, we'll fix this. Let me get Lucy settled, and I'll bring back a broom and a garbage bag."

After a hug, a lollipop and her favorite TV show, *Dora the Explorer*, Lucy was as good as new. I brought the supplies to Garrett who was sitting dazed on the couch.

"She wants to showcase the cats," he said.

"There must be dozens of cats here, let's take one from the cabinet and move things around. She'll never notice a thing."

"Yes, she will. You don't know what she's like," Garrett said in terror. I was beginning to know what she was like.

"Look, we just have to stick together on this. There was no panther. Repeat after me, Garrett. There was no panther."

"There was no panther," he said without conviction.

"Very good. Now stick to the story, and we'll be fine. She'll be here any minute. I'm gonna run upstairs and get dressed."

Garrett nodded. I hated his decorating, but I felt sorry for the guy.

Rachel, David and the photographer showed up twenty minutes later. Garrett had pulled himself together, thank God, and Lucy was asleep on the couch in the den, her life of crime having worn her out. After the obligatory hugs and *sweeties*, I escaped to the kitchen. The photographer clicked away. Then I heard Rachel say, "Garrett, did you move the cats?"

"Um, I, ah, I don't think so," he said. I hurried to the great room to provide back up.

"The lion was definitely not in the front. Do you remember, Kate?"

I pretended to look at the coffee table very hard before saying, "I distinctly remember thinking how much I adored that lion, so it must have been in the front. Why else would I have noticed it?"

"Maybe. I thought the panther was in the front. Where is that panther?"

"Panther?" Garrett squeaked.

"Yes, the panther. Where is it?" Rachel's voice rose an octave.

"Hmmm," I said. "I'm sorry, but I don't remember any panther. Do you mean the leopard?"

"No."

"How about the cheetah?"

"No."

"You must have left the panther at the shop," I said.

"Nooo," Rachel wailed. "We can't have the shoot without the panther. David, you'll have to go back and get it."

David, who had been watching from the couch, stood. "Rachel, the room is beautiful without the panther. No one will notice. I think we've taken up enough of Kate's time. Why don't we finish up here?" I loved David.

"Of course, you're right, darling," she said, backtracking. Rachel might have the mouth, but David clearly wore the pants in the Finley family. "Let's just plump the pillows and finish up." Rachel had almost finished when she held up a satin pillow in horror. "What is this?" she screeched.

In the middle of the pillow was one very distinct, very small handprint.

"Lucy must have touched it with her sticky hands. I'm sorry."

"It's ruined! The whole photo shoot is ruined. How could you do this to me, Kate, after all of our hard work?"

"Rachel, look," I said in a reasonable tone of voice, "I'm sorry, but I have a small child and sometimes things like this happen. You must remember what it's like to have small children?"

"Our children were well-behaved!"

I tried a different tack. "Why don't we turn the pillow over? No one will be able to see it then."

"That's not the point!"

"Rachel, turn the pillow over and let's get this done," David said with authority.

"Fine! I don't care anymore." Rachel flung the pillow on the floor. "You finish up, I'll be waiting in the car!" She stomped out on her twig legs and slammed the front door.

I gave the boys a sympathetic smile as I removed myself from the room. The photographer took his final photos and then the Finley moving men lifted the Liberace piano and carried it away. Lucy and I were finally left in peace with our new jungle cat friends.

Chapter 3

I updated my resume in between *Gold Coast Wives* tapings, rounds of Go Fish with Lucy, and screening my mother-in-law's calls. Since my show stipend wouldn't last forever, I sent my resume to at least twenty of my top industry contacts in addition to several head hunters I'd used over the years. I also called my former clients. None of them were in the position to hire any in-house lawyers, but several promised to keep me in mind. I even scheduled a lunch with the hiring partner at my former rival firm, Kadden Fritz, and although the lunch was quite pleasant, he'd made it clear that in this environment, without a roster of clients, Kadden couldn't even consider hiring me.

Still undeterred, I set up a meeting with Handler Associates, one of the top legal head hunters in New York, and arranged to meet Shari Gruber, my friend from Fowler Sherman, for a late lunch afterward. Wearing a navy blue Armani suit and the diamond stud earrings Jim had given me on our fifth anniversary, I marched into Handler's offices on Madison Avenue. Kyle Madden, one of their top consultants, greeted me with enthusiasm, as well he should have--the commissions he'd earned from Fowler Sherman under my watch had probably paid for his beach house on Fire Island.

"Kate, you look wonderful! It's great to see you."

"You too, Kyle," I said as I sunk into a plush floral couch. "I assume you've been busy."

"To tell you the truth, two years ago I would have killed for the pedigree of candidates I'm seeing now." Kyle ran his hands through his thinning blond hair. "People such as yourself. It's frustrating there is so little to offer at the moment."

"What did you think of my resume? Any suggestions?"

"It's obviously outstanding. But the positions I have right now are for junior associates, nothing at all suitable for someone of your caliber."

"What about GateWay Capital? I heard that Mel Kasmen is retiring, so there should be an opening there. I would have called them myself, but I don't have any contacts at GateWay. Don't you represent them?"

"We do." Kyle looked somewhat uncomfortable. "I don't think it would be right for you."

"What do you mean? It would be perfect."

"They're represented by John Coleman of Kadden Fritz."

"Yes, but surely with his book of business, John wouldn't be interested in an in-house position."

"True, but there's no way Kadden Fritz would allow you to work for one of their clients."

"How do you know? I met with Kadden last week."

"And did Kadden offer you a job?" Kyle asked.

"No. Given the environment they said they weren't hiring."

"That's bull. I placed a '92 Cornell grad there as a service partner last week, and he didn't have a tenth of your experience."

"I don't understand."

"Kate, I've known you for years and you know I respect you enormously, but you and Barry Reiman haven't made too many friends among the hedge fund bar."

"Well, it's a competitive business."

"True, but you and Barry were particularly aggressive. The other law firms didn't exactly appreciate it when you stole their top associates."

I had to admit that when I stole Martina Campbell, one of Kadden Fritz's top associates, I had felt a little guilty. Given Martina's role in my firing, that bit of plunder had bitten me in the ass. Despite my niggling conscience, I said with a bravado I didn't exactly feel, "Please, Kyle, everyone does it."

"Yes, but not to the degree you did."

"So what you're saying is that Kadden Fritz and the other law firms are going deliberately out of their way to ensure I don't find a new position because I recruited a few associates? You make it sound like a conspiracy."

"Maybe not deliberately, but people are dealing with this market crisis and no one knows what 2009 will bring." He looked at me through stylish wire glasses. "It's not that I think people are having meetings and collectively plotting against you. What I do think is there aren't a lot of slices of the pie to go around right now, and if they can keep a slice for themselves and stick it to a former rival, they'll do it."

"So what do you suggest? That I apply for an opening at McDonald's?"

"I'm not saying that. I think you should lie low, let this blow over. People have short memories and once the market rights itself there'll be so much work around that everyone will forget their petty gripes and snap someone like you right up."

"And until then? What am I supposed to do?" Besides embarrassing myself on cable TV.

"Don't you have a little boy? Enjoy your time with him, and we'll regroup in the spring."

I saw there was no point in continuing the conversation. I also wanted to maintain whatever dignity I had left by not revealing the precarious state of my finances. So I said, "Thank you for your candor, Kyle," with what I hoped was a confident smile. "I'm sure it wasn't easy to tell me this."

"Really, Kate, don't worry. We'll find you something. It's just going to take time to find the right opportunity." Kyle complimented me some more on my skills and such, but really, I'd stopped listening. All I wanted to do was escape his stuffy office and meet my friend Shari at the diner for a greasy cheeseburger deluxe.

It took about ten minutes to walk to the Midtown Diner on 57th. The gruff head waiter shepherded me to my usual small booth in the back and brought me a Diet Coke with lemon, without my even asking. It was comforting to be back in my regular lunch place, wearing my subdued work clothes and tasteful jewelry. It felt right.

I sipped my Diet Coke and remembered the summer I'd met Shari. At that time, Fowler Sherman's Hedge Fund group had consisted of Barry Reiman and an owlish fifty-two-year-old tax lawyer named Joel Gittleman, and was part of the larger Asset Management group reporting into Ken Shine. Barry and Joel had shared a dark, desolate corridor on the fifth floor, next to the word processing department. I'd been given an office between them that I shared with another junior lawyer, Shari Gruber. We had both been completing our final rotation until we had to pick a specialty.

Shari was a nice, if somewhat nervous, girl from Forest Hills, Queens, who had recently married her high school boyfriend, a podiatrist. Shari had hoped to win a spot in Asset Management and take advantage of its relatively more humane hours and start producing baby Grubers the following year. I'd hoped to win a spot with the more high-powered Mergers and Acquisitions group and had been putting in my time in the sleepy Asset Management department. I'd planned to coast through the summer and spend my weekends at my Hamptons share house until I could set the world on fire at M-and-A in the fall. Shari and I, both for very different reasons, had looked forward to quiet summer days filled with updating prospectuses, attending board meetings and writing the occasional research memo.

Two weeks into my Asset Management rotation, Barry had stormed into my office. Shari had been attending a board meeting with Ken Shine, so I was alone and listening to my little clock radio while marking up yet another mutual fund prospectus.

"You," Barry Reiman had shouted. "What are you doing?"

"I'm working on the Horizon fund prospectus," I'd said, a bit startled.

"I need you in my office right now and turn off that goddamn radio! I can hear it in my office." I'd felt like saying I could usually hear him yelling at his wife and making dinner plans with his mistress. Of course I'd said nothing other than, "Marc Greenstein needs this document tomorrow."

"Give it to that other mouse, and get in my office!" And with that, Barry had left my office.

I'd understood why Barry was hidden away on this dark corridor, sharing a floor with the accounts receivable department and word processing. No one in their right mind would have voluntarily sat anywhere near this man. We'd worked with the radio on because it was the only way we could block out the volume next door. I hadn't minded the screaming before, since it hadn't been targeted at me, but it had nearly driven poor sensitive Shari out of her mind. I think that was why she'd volunteered to take the minutes at Ken's board meetings--it had kept her off the fifth floor.

I had left Shari a note asking her to review the Horizon prospectuses. I'd grabbed a pen and a yellow legal pad, the tools of the trade for all young associates, taken a deep breath and entered the lunatic asylum that was Barry's office. As I'd opened the door to Barry's wood-paneled, partner size office, a ream of paper hit me. "That prick Mike Templeton apparently can't spare an M and A associate to work on my client's merger, so you'll have to do. Arnie Williams is merging his firm with a small arbitrage shop based in Greenwich to form a new advisory firm, Infinity Capital. I need a complete set of merger and related documents by tomorrow at five o'clock the latest. And don't bother telling me it's your three month anniversary or your mommy's birthday, because I really don't care."

"What's the client matter number?"

"How the hell should I know! Go ask Stacey outside." And with that I had been dismissed.

Shari had returned and was dutifully working on the Horizon documents. She'd looked up and whispered, "I can't believe Ken assigned you to one of Barry's deals. The partners usually don't let him near the rotation associates, you know, because he's a...a..."

"A raving maniac!"

"Shush, these walls are thin."

"You know what, Shari, I really don't care. I'll just give him his document tomorrow and hopefully be done with him. I'm certainly not going to skulk around here for the next three months quivering in fear that Barry's going to yell at me. Let him hear me call him a maniac, I'm sure I'm not the first."

"I would die. I would just die if it were me."

"I have no intention of dying. My share house is having a Fourth of July party this weekend, and I plan to be there," and with that I'd turned on my radio and gotten to work.

The next day I'd left the drafts on Barry's chair by two and then headed out to my share house where I had a spectacular weekend. It was a good thing I had enjoyed it because it was the last I was to see of East Hampton that summer. Barry had been so impressed with my merger documents he'd convinced Ken Shine to have me assigned to him exclusively for the remainder of my Asset Management rotation.

Lucky me.

By the end of the summer, Barry had promised me the world, moon and the stars in addition to an early partnership track if I would agree to join him in the Hedge Funds group. Shari had joined Ken in Asset Management and the rest, as they say, was history.

Shari bustled in and gave me a White Linen-infused embrace. "Kate, I love the hair!"

"Thanks, a bit of a makeover." Chris had cut off about six inches of split ends before we'd started taping. "I'm even wearing makeup. Are you impressed?"

"Very. What did Kyle have to say?" Shari asked as she settled into her seat.

"My resume looks great, blah blah blah. There are no openings, blah, blah blah."

"That was helpful." She placed her Blackberry beside her Diet Coke. Shari gestured to the device. "Sorry, I'm expecting a response from the SEC."

"No problem. Would you believe I actually miss that thing?"

Shari shook her head. "Sometimes I want to throw it out the window!"

The waiter landed our cheeseburger deluxe platters on the table.

"Kyle did say something that surprised me," I said, and filled in Shari on Kyle's conspiracy theory.

"Honestly, it doesn't sound that far-fetched to me, Kate. Barry's made a lot of enemies over the years, and I suppose you bear the taint of association," Shari said matter-of-factly.

"Bad enough I had to deal with that lunatic while I was working with him."

"Come on, Kate, that lunatic made you one of the youngest partners in Fowler Sherman history. You knew what he was when you first hooked up with him. You rode on Barry's coat tails for years. It's a bit disingenuous of you to complain now."

Wow. In all our years of complaining about Barry and Ken, Shari had never been this blunt before. I wondered how long she'd thought this.

"True," I replied, because what else could I say, "but I worked hard to establish my own name, independent of Barry."

"As my grandmother always said, 'Lie down with dogs, you get up with fleas.' What you have to do now is get rid of your Barry fleas."

"Easier said than done."

"Well, maybe Kyle is right. Take some time off, take a trip. You said it did wonders for Jim. Did he enjoy his trip?"

"He had the time of his life." I wasn't about to disclose my marital and financial problems to Shari now.

"We might take the boys to England and Ireland next year. They love golf," Shari said, finishing her burger.

"Coffee, ladies?"

Shari looked at her Blackberry. "Sweetie, do you mind? My SEC response is in. I really have to get back."

"Not at all. Go. Go."

"Next time, I swear, I'll have more time. Maybe we can have dinner." Over the years Shari and I had at times suggested dinners, weekend shopping trips, etc. They'd never happened. We were work friends, and now that we no longer worked together, I realized the friendship was unlikely to survive beyond annual holiday cards and the occasional email. After my father had retired from the fire department, he'd surprised us when he cut ties with many of the still active firemen. "When you're in, you're the best. When you're out, you're a pest," he had said. Looks like he had been right.

"Sure." I made an attempt at a warm smile. "Plus, I'm sure I'll be back in the city soon."

"Great!" Shari leaned in to kiss me on the cheek. "Keep your chin up, kiddo. Things will work out."

"Right," I said to Shari's back as she scurried out of the diner.

Sure they would.

I walked to the overpriced parking garage where I'd parked and was about to hand the attendant my ticket, when I stopped, took out my cellphone and called Deirdre.

"Hey, it's me. Can you get out tonight?"

"Why?"

"Do you want to meet me in the city for some drinks? I just can't go home and face the jungle cats in my great room."

"Sure. I'm up for it."

"Great. Why don't you give Angela a call. I'll meet you at the Monkey Bar."

"Is everything okay, Kate?"

"It will be after a few Cosmos." Cosmos were so 90s, but after I got married my knowledge of cool drinks atrophied.

I had parked in the parking garage below Fowler Sherman, so I walked across Park Avenue to the Monkey Bar on East 54th Street. Since Vanity Fair editor Graydon Carter had taken over the place and refurbished it, the Monkey Bar had become a *beautiful people* bar, full of models, celebrities and various levels of New York socialites. Before the Graydon invasion, the Monkey Bar had been a mainstay of Fowler Sherman's client luncheons and after work get-togethers, and I still knew the maitre'd and most of the bartenders. Being slightly over forty and slightly overweight, I got a few looks from the fabulous crowd when I was greeted with a big smile by Simon the bartender--the benefits of being a good tipper. I snagged the coveted corner seat at the bar where Simon poured me an extra strong, ice cold Cosmo. I observed the glitterati and was on my third killer Cosmo when Deirdre and Angela joined me at the bar. Deirdre was wearing her standard "night on the town" uniform of a silk blouse and a slim black pencil skirt. Angela was decked out in a skin-tight leather miniskirt, her long, curly, blue-black hair even bigger than usual.

"Drinks in the afternoon. When was the last time we did that?" Angela enveloped me in a big hug and almost smothered me with her thick mane. "I was telling Dee in the cab from Penn, I think I like the new unemployed Kit Kat. You're much more fun."

"Yeah, after the meeting I had this morning it looks like I may be the new 'fun' Kate for quite some time. It'll sure be fun when I run out of money and am living in a homeless shelter. Or selling my blood for five bucks. Or..."

"Or starring in the second season of *Gold Coast Wives*," Angela gushed.

"I think I'd rather sell my blood." I waved for Simon to come over. "I think we definitely need a round of drinks."

Angela preened on the high bar stool, looking around the bar to see if anyone noticed her. "Have you heard from Jim?"

"This is all Jim's fault. I don't know what possessed him to buy those stocks on margin. I swear, if he wasn't off with Crocodile Dundee, I would wring his neck."

"He's still not coming back?"

"Oh, he needs to think. About his life. About what he wants to do. I think he's in Thailand now."

"Isn't that where they have all those prostitution tours?" Angela asked. Deirdre poked her in the arm. I looked at the two of them sitting side by side and was suddenly reminded of our days on the school bus to Queen of the Rosary Academy. Angela had entertained us with her arcane knowledge of various perverted sexual matters, matters that certainly would've shocked the good sisters at Queen of the Rosary.

And now here we were, so many years later, discussing my husband and his possible interest in Thai prostitutes. The vodka must have hit me because I started to laugh. And laugh. Two Eastern European anorexic model-types stared at me, but I didn't care. And neither did Angela and Deirdre who joined in.

"I think you're drunk, Miss Kate. What would Elaine say if she could see you now?" Angela asked.

"She'd probably tell me to 'act natural.' Okay, enough about me and my problems. I'm boring myself now. Let's talk about you, Angie. Has Jerry reinstated your credit cards yet? How are the owls?"

"Wait," Deirdre interrupted, "how did you get started on this owl kick anyway?"

"It started when Jerry canceled my American Express card," Angela said as though she had lost a limb. Angela without her platinum card was like peanut butter without jelly. "Jerry was always complaining about the lamps in our bedroom, he said he couldn't see anything. One day, I walked past Finley's, and I saw the most perfect lamps. They were incredible-- hand blown glass, silky lamp shades the perfect shade of green to match my duvet cover. So I went in, bought the lamps and took them straight home. And Jerry of course loved them. But that stupid salesgirl left the tags on, and before he went to sleep he noticed the price and went nuts. He said the lamps were too expensive, can you believe it?

"How much were they?" Deirdre asked.

"Let's just say, a lot."

"Come on, how much?" she persisted.

"Twenty-five hundred."

"Twenty-five hundred dollars for a pair of lamps!" my sister squealed.

"Per lamp. Five thousand for the pair."

"You're insane, Ang. I think I furnished my whole house for five grand," Deirdre said.

"Anyway, of course one thing led to another and the next morning when I went to use my Amex to order a bracelet, the card was gone. Along with my Bloomingdale's and Sak's charge cards. Alls he left me with was a MasterCard with a lousy five-thousand dollar limit and a Gap charge card for the kids' clothes. Can you imagine?"

"Jerry usually doesn't care how much you spend," I said. "What's really going on?"

"Oh, who knows. He keeps going on and on about the recession and slow-downs in home renovations, but his office seems busy enough to me. All of a sudden he's on my ass about every little thing. Well, I told him, I had enough. I told him he could stick the lousy card. I could make my own money!"

"By selling gold cats?"

"They're not cats, Dee. They're owls. Owls are hot now, everyone knows that."

"No offense, Angela, but the last job you had was at Burger King, and I seem to remember you were fired after a month. How are you going to run your own business? You didn't even graduate from Nassau Community College," Deirdre said, always the black cloud of reason.

"Oh, you're such a downer. Jerry runs his own business, and he barely graduated from high school--*public* high school. Why can't I run a business?"

"You know what, Angela? I think your owls are going to be a big hit. Who says you have to go to college to be a success? Look at me. Now let's order champagne and drink to, what's the name of your company again?" I asked.

"Angela Rosetti Fine Jewelry," she preened.

"Here's to that. Simon, champagne please."

After we'd each finished two glasses and Angela had filled us in on her marketing plan, which sounded a bit sketchy to be honest, I weaved my way over to the ladies room. Once there, I stared into the mirror and saw that my curly hair was wilder than usual. I was trying to get a comb through my red mop when Julia Reiman, Barry's wife, walked through the ladies room door, outfitted from head to toe in Tory Burch, her shiny bobbed hair perfectly in place.

"Kate! What are you doing here?" she asked giving me a hearty hug.

"I'm having a few drinks with friends."

"Why aren't you in Denver with Barry at the American Asset Managers Conference?"

"That conference was last summer in Boston."

"No, no, that's not possible."

"Julia, I'm sorry but I've spoken at that conference for the last five years, and it's always in June. I don't know where Barry is, but he's certainly not speaking at that conference."

"Are you sure?"

"Look, Julia," I said heading toward the door, "I'm the last person who would know what Barry is up to."

"What are you talking about, Kate? You work right down the hall from him," Julia said with a smile, as if talking to a toddler.

Oh, to hell with it. "He fired me weeks ago. Didn't you know?"

"Fired? That can't be right. You must be mistaken. You're a partner, you can't be fired."

"Tell that to Barry and the Executive Committee. I've got to get back to my friends. Why don't you butter up his secretary, Stacey? She knows his every move and can tell you what he's been up to. Plus, she's quite susceptible to bribery."

"Bribery?" Julia asked, looking confused.

I opened the ladies room door. "Sure, bribery. After all," I smiled, "that's how the first Mrs. Reiman found out about you." With that, I hustled back to the bar and gathered the girls and their assorted outerwear before Julia could catch up with me.

* * * *

Next morning I woke to the sound of Dee's grinding teeth. My neck ached from the too high foam hotel pillow, and I felt queasy. I untangled myself from the expensive sheets and stumbled into a large bathroom suite, one with a phone next to the toilet and everything. Where the hell were we? After I splashed water on my face and rubbed off the mascara that ringed my bloodshot eyes, I picked up the bathroom phone.

"Peninsula Hotel, may I help you?" a too loud and too cheerful employee said.

"Can you please send up coffee and three orders of bacon and eggs?" I croaked. That would probably cost a hundred bucks. Whose idea was it to check into the Peninsula anyway? I hoped to God I hadn't put it on my credit card.

"Yes, Ms. Rosetti. Breakfast will be there in twenty minutes."

I tore through Deirdre's purse by the bathroom door, looking for Advil. Her purse always weighed a ton because she's quite the Girl Scout and carries at least three different pain killers, along with an assortment of other necessities: band aids, clear nail polish, breath mints, hair spray, pens. I swallowed four Advil, crawled over to my bed and prayed for the pounding in my head to stop.

I must have fallen back asleep because before I knew it Angela was waving a hot cup of coffee under my nose.

"Wake up, dancing queen!" She looked like she'd just left the beauty parlor--she even had on fresh lipstick.

I grabbed the mug. "How did we get here?"

"Don't you remember running out of the Monkey Bar?"

Oh God. Julia Reiman. Had I really told that poor woman her husband was probably cheating on her?

"Yes, I remember. It gets a bit fuzzy after that." I winced as Angela opened the heavy brocade drapes.

"Well, we spent twenty minutes walking around in circles looking for Au Bar. You swore you wouldn't go home without one dance." Oh dear God, Au Bar was a heinous, Euro trashy bar Glenn Meyers used to drag me to after late nights in the office. I hadn't been there since 1999.

"Did we make it there?"

"Unfortunately. We finally figured out that they'd renamed the place. Dee and I paid our forty dollar cover charges, but the bouncers wouldn't let you in."

"You owe me forty bucks," Dee chimed in without opening her eyes.

"Why wouldn't they let me in?"

"Well, uh..."

I lifted my head. "The club doesn't let in fat chicks over forty. Is that it? You two made the cut, and I didn't. Don't bother denying it. What happened next?"

"You sat down in the doorway and cried."

"Please, please tell me I didn't."

"Oh yes you did," Deirdre said, now fully awake and seeming to enjoy my humiliation a little too much. "You sat down, cried and told them you wouldn't leave without one dance. Some guy named Benoit who recognized you convinced the doorman to let you in." The only Benoit I knew was a French Canadian third year associate at Fowler Sherman.

"I think he slipped the doorman a fifty," added Angela.

"Did we go in?"

"Did we go in? We were there two hours. First, you told your friend Benoit he was the smartest lawyer at Fowler Sherman." Okay, I guess it had been Benoit the third year. "Then you proceeded to do shots with him and his friend Ignacio, who you complimented on his soulful eyes."

"What does soulful eyes even mean?" piped in Deirdre.

"You danced on a raised platform," continued Angela.

"Oh no, I didn't dance, did I?" I generally looked like a giraffe having a seizure when I danced.

"Oh, yes you did. You danced to some Moroccan love song with your new best friend Ignacio on the platform until..."

"Until what? Until I fell?" I rubbed my ankles, searching for the all too familiar sprain.

"No, you didn't exactly fall this time."

"Then what? What did I do?"

"You tried to take off your bra while dancing with Ignacio because you said you were too hot."

I hid my head under the blanket. "I didn't."

"You didn't quite take it off because you somehow clocked Ignacio in the eye with your elbow and knocked him off the little stage."

Peeking out, I asked, "Is he okay?"

"I don't know, the bouncers threw us out after that. Jack the cameraman tried to convince the bouncers to let us stay. We got kicked out anyway," Angela said.

"Wait a second. Jack, the cameraman from *Gold Coast Wives*? What was he doing there?"

"I guess I might have mentioned to Chris we were going out for drinks," Angela said.

"Yeah, and she just *happened* to call Chris and let him know when we left the Monkey Bar," tattled Deirdre.

"So my drunken dance was caught on tape? Wonderful. But why didn't we take a car home after we got thrown out? How did we end up here?"

"You wanted a nightcap at your favorite hotel bar," Angela said.

"Why didn't you just take me home?"

"Are you kidding me?" my sister asked. "I haven't been out in the city in over two years. I wasn't about to go home before ten!"

"All this happened by ten?"

"Well, we started drinking at the Monkey Bar by five. Make that by three for you. Anyway," Angela continued, sounding like a newscaster, "we went to the bar downstairs, and at that point you seemed to sober up a bit and we even got some coffee into you. Until..."

"Until? Until what?"

"Until Billy Jones walked in the bar."

"Oh my God!" I screeched, hurting my own head. "We saw Billy Jones?" Billy Jones was an eighties pop star from Long Island. To say I grew up obsessed with him would be an understatement.

"We didn't only see Billy Jones."

"Did we talk to Billy Jones?"

"I suppose you could call it that."

Deirdre cut in and said, "You walked up to him and told him you lost your virginity while listening to his first album."

"No!"

"And you sang him a medley of his greatest hits," Angela said, trying not to laugh.

"Not just the chorus, you sang the verses too," Deirdre added.

"What did he do?"

Angela couldn't keep a straight face. "He said you had a wonderful voice. And then you, Billy and his friend went to the end of the bar and did shots together."

"And there was more singing," Deirdre said with a giggle.

"By me or by him?" I asked.

"You sang a duet."

"You have to be making this up," I said, although I kind of remembered singing with someone last night.

"Ask the bartender if you don't believe us. Or you could watch it on TV."

"Then we came back to the room?" I dared to hope.

"Not before you told Billy that your husband had left you, and you were now available."

"I did not say that! Please stop. Just stop." I hid my head in the too high foam pillow.

"The weird thing is, Kit Kat," Angela said, "I think he was kind of into you. After all, he did kiss you on the lips before he left. Which was also caught by Jack the cameraman."

"I hate you. I hate you both."

"I'm serious. If his friend hadn't finally dragged him away, maybe you would be the next Mrs. Billy Jones."

"He's already married to some teenager," I said. I probably knew too much about Billy Jones. Pretty sad.

"I think they got divorced. Anyway, I emailed Jerry this picture. Wanna see?" Angela showed us the picture from her phone of me and Billy singing together.

I looked like the jolly green giant on acid, towering over poor Billy. In the photo I was pretending a swizzle stick was a microphone. Nice.

"Jerry thought it was so funny that he agreed to pay our hotel bill."

"If Jim does leave me for good, I'm joining a convent. I clearly can't handle the single life anymore."

After we checked out and Angela covered our over five-hundred dollar tab--thank you Jerry--we walked over to the parking garage on Park Avenue and piled into my X3. Thankfully, there were no cameras to catch us in all our hung-over glory. Channel 45 was probably too cheap to pay for a hotel room for Jack the cameraman. We weren't out of the midtown tunnel before Angela began to whine about my CD collection--apparently she was now into hip hop and my Norah Jones CDs didn't cut it--and Deirdre complained about having to sit in the back seat. It could have been 1984. I almost expected them to start copying my algebra homework.

After dropping off Angela and Dee and picking up Lucy from my parents' house, I headed home. While Lucy ate macaroni and cheese, I turned on my laptop and decided to send an email to NYJimmy66.

Dear Husband,

Hope you're enjoying yourself in Australia or Thailand or wherever the hell you are. Your child still has a roof over her head, no thanks to you since you managed to gamble away our nest egg. I'll probably need to sell your clothes in order to meet next month's mortgage payment. Your golf clubs were sold last month.

I did, however, kiss Billy Jones at the Peninsula Hotel last night, so things are looking up for me in the romance department.

Watch out for crocodiles.

Your loving wife,

Kate--in case you forgot

Asshole.

Chapter 4

One hour. All I had to do was make it through one hour without spilling anything or insulting a Wife. Surely to God, even I could handle that.

I carefully tottered to the Halesite Yacht Club entrance on the black stilettos I thought Chris had given me as punishment. I couldn't stop touching my unfamiliar pin-straight locks. Chris had almost burned out his blow dryer while straightening my hair, but it was worth it to be able to shake my hair like a supermodel. After the makeup debacle, Elaine must have read Chris the riot act because he pulled out all the stops to make me look as much like a sex kitten as was possible. Well, a pleasantly plump sex kitten. The straight hair was paired with smoky eye makeup and an exquisite forest green empire-waisted cocktail dress that hid a multitude of sins. It was a shame I was staying only an hour, but I was sure the Griffin clan awaiting me at the Lindenhurst Knights of Columbus hall would appreciate Chris's efforts.

A Channel 45 camera man appeared out of nowhere to film my wobbly ascent up the marble staircase. A uniformed doorman opened the heavy glass doors and as soon as we entered, the cameraman and I were assaulted by the sounds of a discordant string quartet. A tuxedoed waiter handed me a glass of champagne and tried not to look at the camera--I assumed Elaine had given the staff her "act natural" speech. I made my unsteady way to the main ballroom and searched for a corner to hide in as I served my hour-long sentence.

At least two hundred people crowded the small ballroom decorated in the silvers and blues that Pamela favored. The air was heavy with enormous flower arrangements that dwarfed the small tables surrounding the dance floor. The whole effect was rather dizzying. I walked to a small empty table in the back and looked at my watch--only fifty-five more minutes to go.

The crowd was a mix of Don's work colleagues, young publishing types whom I assumed did most of the heavy lifting on Pamela's book, and various minor league North Shore socialites I recognized from *Gold Coast Now*, a semi-annual lifestyle magazine modeled on its Hamptons cousin. From a distance I saw Don speaking with David. Pamela and Rachel were nowhere to be seen. I slowly sipped my champagne.

Some of the young minions set up a dais in the middle of the dance floor, and fifteen minutes later Pamela entered the ballroom and strode to the microphone like a supermodel on the catwalk in her floor-length aquamarine gown.

"Welcome," Pamela said in her husky voice. "Welcome, everyone, to the launch of *Gold Coast Entertaining*!" Pamela was met with polite applause, although looking at her face one would've thought it was a standing ovation. She enthralled the audience with a brief history of her *passion* for entertaining. I looked at my watch, only thirty more minutes to go. Pamela thanked a plethora of ghostwriters, oh sorry, *editorial assistants*, her publicist, her husband. I continued zoning out when the words *Gold Coast Wives* woke me out of my speech-induced stupor.

"My fellow Gold Coast Wives have provided so much support and inspiration for *Gold Coast Entertaining*." What in God's name was she talking about? "I am forever grateful to them. I would love to introduce you to two of my dear Gold Coast Wives friends who have joined me tonight. Rachel Finley and Kate Ryan! Girls come on up here!"

Rachel sashayed up to the dais. I reluctantly made my way through the crowd. The three of us linked arms while the paparazzi--no, the paid photographers--took our pictures. My mouth hurt from smiling so hard. Neither Rachel nor Pamela looked at me directly, but I assumed this wasn't evident to either the audience or the photographers. Once freed from Pamela's vise-like grip, I escaped to the bar in the back. I looked at my watch, only fifteen more minutes to go.

"Vodka tonic," I told the bartender.

"Gosh, was taking your picture really that bad?" someone asked in a deep rumbling voice.

"With that group it was." I grabbed my drink.

"A pretty group of girls like you? I find it hard to believe."

"We're hardly girls."

"Please, how old can you be? Thirty?" Paul, Don's brother-in-law, asked. Was he joking or just near-sighted?

"That's it, you guessed it. I'm thirty. It's tough leaving your twenties. Takes a lot of getting used to--that's where the alcohol comes in." I took another sip, looked at my watch and saw I had another ten minutes before I could escape. Paul was kind of cute and seemed nice--I decided to keep the snarky comments to a minimum. "So Paul, do you have a last name?"

"I do, actually. Goodman, Paul Goodman. And I'll let you in on a little secret. I'm not exactly old Pamela's favorite person either." Paul smiled. His teeth were a little crooked, but I found it kind of endearing. I was so used to the physical perfection of Jim that it was nice to see a man with a flaw. Much less intimidating.

"What did you do to fall out of Pamela's favor?" I asked as I finished my vodka tonic. I felt my face start to get warm, unsure of whether it was from the alcohol or the strain of keeping up my side of what I thought was a flirtatious conversation. I was definitely rusty in the flirting department.

"Let's just say she thinks I'm a bad influence on Donny. Can I get you another drink?" He motioned for the bartender.

"Now I think you may be a bad influence on me," I said, tossing my model-worthy hair. Someone tapped me on the shoulder.

"I'm here to rescue you," Deirdre said, a little out of breath. "Sorry I'm late. The kids were fighting over the Wii again."

"No problem. Do you want a drink?"

"Drink? I thought you were dying to get out of here."

"I am, but we have time for another drink."

"Yes," said Paul, "you can't abandon me now. Surely you have time for a drink?"

"Unfortunately, we're late as it is. We're going to a surprise birthday party. I'm Kate's sister Deirdre by the way." She offered Paul her hand.

"Oh, sorry, where are my manners," I said with another hair toss. "This is Paul Goodman, Pamela's brother-in-law. Well, sorta brother-in-law." I gave a giggly laugh worthy of an eighth grader.

"Is there any way I can tempt you to stay?" he asked.

"Another time perhaps, Paul." Deirdre firmly took the drink out of my hand. "My husband is waiting in the car."

"Bye now," I said.

"Bye, Kate. It was nice seeing you again." Paul smiled his crooked smile.

We made our way through the crowd, carefully avoiding the other Wives. "You wanted to be rescued, Kate, didn't you?"

"Sure, I don't want to miss Uncle Danny's party."

"You're not interested in that guy, are you?" Deirdre asked with a shudder

"Oh, no."

"Good, because I don't think he's your type."

"Why? What was wrong with him?"

"I don't know. He seemed kind of, oh I don't know, kind of grizzly."

"Grizzly like a bear?" I asked.

"Oh, I don't know. Grizzly like he needed to use some moisturizer."

"Dee," I said with a laugh, "not every man is addicted to Clinique for Men, like Gordon."

"You asked," Deirdre said as she pushed against the heavy glass door to exit. The doormen seemed to have disappeared along with the cameras.

"It doesn't matter anyway. I'm still a married woman."

"And let's hope you stay that way." My sister always had a soft spot for Jim, and I knew she hoped we'd work things out. "Hey, did Dad tell you who Uncle Sean is bringing to the party?"

"Sean has a date?" I asked, shocked.

"Your best friend."

"No."

"Yes. Peg Ryan."

My uncle Sean, a widower, joined us most holidays and had gotten to know Peg quite well. Surprisingly, they'd really hit it off, and the whole family thought it was funny that the gentle, hulking Sean seemed enamored by the small, quarrelsome Peg. To date, she had always rebuffed his advances. I guess after all these years he'd worn her down.

"Oh dear God. The only good thing about Jim's leaving was not having to deal with his mother. Is Mom pissed?"

"She doesn't know yet. Dad was too chicken to tell her," Deirdre said with a laugh.

"Let's hurry up. I don't want to miss this!"

Chapter 5

We had a week and a half off before the final flurry of *Gold Coast Wives* activity would begin again. The spa day at Tina's house was scheduled for next Friday, with the LICKs Ball to follow the next night. It was a relief not to worry about my hair or makeup or be concerned about the hidden cameras being randomly turned on. I knew Harry had sworn he'd only filmed during scheduled taping hours, but I suspected the remote cameras went on more often, including when either my hair was standing on end or I was bitching about Pamela.

I surfed through my emails. None from NYJimmy66, but I did receive one from Shari entitled *Way to Go Dancing Queen!* It read:

One of the third year associates in litigation sent this to someone in my department, who forwarded it to me. Glad to see you're making the most of your time off!!

The attached picture showed me dancing with Ignacio, towering over him, with my hands shaking over my head.

I emailed back. "Has everyone seen this, do you think?"

Within ten minutes she replied, "Oh, absolutely."

The thought of Barry and Martina laughing over this made me sick.

"One night. I went out one night," I moaned.

Deirdre came by later that day to help me rearrange the great room. She cleared the room of all things shiny and feline, save for one little lion I'd actually grown attached to. She also stripped the room of the electric blue tapestries and any other stray accoutrements that made my head hurt. Once she was finished, the great room looked quite elegant, much how I imagined French country was supposed to be, without the twist. I boxed up the removed items to return to Finley's. Deirdre promised to drop them off at the store during the spa day, so I wouldn't have to face either Rachel or Garrett. I know, I'm a wimp.

After our hard work, Deirdre and I had to have the obligatory cup of tea and piece of cake, of course. As I cut Dee her second slice of pound cake, she asked, "Kate, when all this TV stuff is done, what are you really going to do about Jim?"

"Nothing. There's nothing for me to do. He's made his choice, now let him live with it. My friend Karen Rice practices family law. Once I find out where he is, Karen'll serve him with divorce papers."

"That's it? You're not going to fight for him? How can you be so cold? I know you still love him."

"It's not a matter of me not loving him, Dee. If I allowed myself to think about him and how much I love him, I'd never get out of bed in the morning. I have a child to support and a house to run. I don't have that luxury."

"That's bullshit, Kate. You have been strangely calm ever since he left. I know if Gordon ever left me, I would be a complete basket case. I certainly wouldn't have the energy to be on TV shows and flirt with strangers at parties."

"That's not fair. I've done what I had to in order to keep my head above water."

"I know but still. You have to admit the way you've reacted to all this is odd, to say the least. I would be devastated if it was Gordon. Much as he annoys me at times, the thought of losing him...I couldn't take it."

"I guess that's the difference between us," I said. "You couldn't imagine Gordon leaving. I'm being honest with myself--it was always in the back of my mind that Jim might leave."

"Really? Why? You never said anything about it before."

"Come on, weren't you all a little surprised when you first met Jim? That someone who looked like him would go out with someone like me?"

She wouldn't meet my eyes. "Oh, don't be ridiculous. You act like you're Quasimodo."

"No, Dee, you want me to be honest, so you be honest too. Didn't you think that? Just a little?"

"Okay, maybe a little," she admitted. She was silent then, and we both sat and drank our tea. As I chewed on my cake I remembered that fateful Memorial Day weekend. I had been made partner, and Glenn Meyers had invited me out to East Hampton to celebrate. On Sunday night, he had hosted a huge party with a local reggae band set up on the basketball court. I'd been relaxing on a lounge chair by the tiki bar, drinking one of Glenn's deadly rum Bahama Mamas, when I saw him.

Tall, broad shoulders, thick dark hair, fair skin. He looked so much like Prince Charming in *Cinderella*, it was ridiculous. Bolstered by my three Bahama Mamas, I'd walked over to him and, in perfect hostess mode, had asked him if he needed a drink. Although he'd already had a full bottle of beer in his hand, he followed me over to the tiki bar where Glenn poured us both shots. We'd talked for the next two hours about I don't know what, and had ended the night kissing to *No Woman No Cry*.

Clearly Jim Ryan had never received the Manhattan Single Heterosexual Male Manual because he called me at my office the next Tuesday at ten. I'd disregarded my copy of The Rules and, after having hit my local overpriced salon for a blow-out, met him that night at a perfect first date restaurant on Park Avenue South. Over a bottle of pinot grigio and a shared plate of tiramisu, Jim had told me about his childhood growing up in East Moriches, a small rural town on a desolate stretch of Long Island's east end. I'd regaled Jim with stories of my illustrious Irish dancing career, which consisted primarily of tripping and twisted ankles. We'd talked about our families. He'd told me about being the henpecked youngest of five and only son. We'd talked about all the things one talks about and can never quite remember when sitting across from the person one suspects they may spend the rest of their life with.

Like me, Jim was hardworking and career focused. Unlike me, Jim was quiet, almost introspective. City living was hard for him. He'd never embraced the noise and the crowds. His dream was to live quietly in a house by the sea.

Jim and I both came from similar Irish Catholic backgrounds, and once my family had met Jim they were in love. Once Peg Ryan had met me, she didn't hate me as much as Jim's previous girlfriends, which Jim had seen as progress. No one was really surprised when we got engaged the following March and married in September. For the next eight years, James Francis Ryan really had been my Prince Charming.

"Kate, I'll admit I was surprised. But that was before I got to know him and saw how much he loved you. He held your hand through four miscarriages. How can you doubt that he loves you?"

"I know he loved me. I know we had a good marriage. Still, I think there was always a part of me that never really believed it could last. That never really believed I could hold onto someone like Jim, someone so perfect. I think, on some level, I always expected him to leave. Maybe that's why I didn't completely fall apart when it actually happened."

Deirdre took my hand. "Kate, you didn't deserve this. No one deserves this."

"I just thank God I had you and Mom and Dad. And even Angela and her crazy owls. I don't know what I would've done without you."

Later, I wished Dee hadn't asked me about Jim before the end of the taping schedule. I was having a hard enough time keeping it together as it was. While at first it felt good to voice all the thoughts that I'd kept unsaid, even to myself, saying them out loud had made it all too real to me.

Sometimes denial is a good thing, especially when you're in reality TV hell.

Chapter 6

"Hey, what are you doing tonight?"

"Dee's dragging me to a scrapbooking meeting in her church basement."

"Boring!" Angela trilled.

"Yeah, well, welcome to my life."

"I have a much better idea. Why don't you and Deirdre blow off the church basement thingy and come to my launch party tonight."

"Launch of what?"

"My jewelry line, silly."

"And you're having a launch party tonight?"

"Yeah, tonight. Chrissy and I just came up with the idea. My Uncle Anthony offered me his restaurant in Cold Spring Harbor. You in or what?"

"Sure, I'm in. Who else is going?"

"I don't know yet, I'm still inviting people. I called you first."

Odd that she would call me first. We weren't that close. But anything would be better than hanging out with middle-aged ladies in sweatpants playing with construction paper. "Fantastic. I'll call Dee."

"Great, I knew I could count on you! Now wear something fun and make sure you work your owls!"

I laughed. "Okay, I'll work my owls."

Surprisingly, it took some convincing to make Dee give up her scrapbooking night. Apparently she'd bought a cricket--whatever that was--and wanted to try it out.

My mother agreed to come over to my place and watch Lucy. She almost never volunteered to babysit when she was particularly pumped about a book. I must have sounded particularly pathetic.

Grace came at five to give me a chance to shower and get ready in peace. While I used the remainder of my expensive anti-frizz serum and searched for an outfit, Mom fed Lucy a dinner of meatloaf, mashed potatoes and spinach--food Lucy wouldn't even look at for me. Lucy was finishing her last spoonful when I came down the stairs wearing the black skirt from one of my Armani suits, a clingy dark red silk sweater and my highest heels. Given my recent weight gain, everything was shorter and tighter than usual. In order to make Angela happy, I'd added the silver owl earrings she had given me. I didn't want to be accused of not working my owls.

"Wow, you look different."

"Different good or different bad?" I asked.

"Angela Mascaro different," she sniffed. My mother had never been a big fan of Angela's.

"When in Rome..."

"Enjoy yourself anyway," she said, opening up her laptop.

"How's it going?"

"I had to stop working on the memoir. Heartland wanted me to make a few changes to *A Pocketful of Gold*."

"When is it due?"

"I got another two month extension, but I want to finish it sooner so I can get back to my autobiography. I'm having a hard time with the Fiona character," she said with a sigh. "My writing group doesn't think she's sympathetic enough."

"Did you try giving her a disability of some sort?" Usually when Grace's, or should I say Penelope's, characters were a little too perfect, she gave them a limp or something not too disfiguring in order to humanize them.

"I tried a nervous tic. I don't know, it doesn't seem to be working."

"Maybe you should try a plot twist. Instead of her winding up with the noble stable boy, you could have her fall for that bastard Lord Cartwright." I put on my coat.

"No, no. That wouldn't work. In the Heartland universe the heroine always winds up with the white knight."

I hugged Lucy. "I should try moving there."

"I told you not to let him take that trip," she said, my mother not being one to resist a good I-told-you-so opportunity.

"And you were right. I won't be too late."

* * * *

Villa Mascaro, Angela's uncle's place, was an upscale Italian restaurant that had started out as a small storefront in a strip mall. It had morphed over the years into a restaurant and an event hall that hosted small weddings, christening parties, and now, jewelry launch parties. As I drove up I saw Angela's Jag, Deirdre's Dodge Caravan and several Channel 45 trucks.

I walked through an ornate onyx and marble hallway where I was directed to the Venetian Banquet Room. As I walked into the Venetian room, I was greeted by the glare of television cameras and an Angela squeal.

"Honey, you made it!"

"Yeah, sorry I'm late. You look, uh, nice."

Angela twirled around in a gold, skin-tight, crystal-encrusted dress. Between the dress and the camera lights, I was blinded. Her hair was teased out several inches from her head, and I thought she was wearing fake eyelashes. On anyone else, this ensemble would be scary, but of course on Angela it looked just right. Well, almost right.

Deirdre, holding a large Margarita, smiled behind her. Wearing yet another variation of her "going out" outfit, same black pencil skirt paired with a dark pink silk blouse, she looked like the sexy, slightly saucy schoolteacher she was.

"What's with the cameras? I didn't think this was a *Gold Coast* event."

Angela ran her fingers through her hair in an attempt to poof it up even more. "It was a little too last minute for this to be an official GCW event. Rachel's away at a furniture convention, and Tina's in Japan shooting a commercial. Chrissy told Elaine how you and I are as close as sisters, so production was able to classify it as one of your *at home* tapings."

"Even though I'm not at home?"

"Yeah, well, whatever. You're here now, so let's have fun!"

Deirdre handed me her Margarita. I took a large sip. "Sure, let's have fun."

"Close as sisters?" Deirdre rolled her eyes. Before I'd met up with her two months ago, I think I had seen Angela a total of four times in the last five years. And before that, I couldn't even say. Not that we were on bad terms or anything, but life had taken us in two very different directions. Me to college, law school and the indentured servitude of Fowler Sherman. Angela into the brawny arms of Jerry Rosetti and Long Island yummy mummyhood. I liked Angela, that's true. We shared high school memories, and Angela always made me smile. Close as sisters? That was a bit of a stretch.

The place was packed with at least one-hundred fifty people. It was hard to believe Angela had really pulled this together in a few days. At least half the people were some type of relative of Angela or Jerry. The other half was a mix of North Shore yummies and Chris's friends from

Channel 45. I even noticed a group of the semi-socialites from Pamela's party and a *Gold Coast Now* reporter. Exposure on Channel 45 and a mention in *Gold Coast Now*--maybe Angela's marketing plan wasn't as sketchy as we'd thought.

Deirdre and I feasted at the raw bar. Angela flitted around the party, so weighed down with owls that she looked a little like a wild life preserve. Chris and his cousin Marco hung out with us for a half hour and even convinced Dee to do a shot of Sambuca. Given my recent humiliation at the Monkey Bar, I tried to stay somewhat sober.

Chris, Marco and Dee joined Angela and Jerry on the small dance floor. I sat next to Jerry's older sister, Annabella, sharing her enormous plate of fried calamari and chatting about her recent divorce. She assured me that the brave new world of online dating was a treasure trove of men who couldn't wait to meet overweight forty-somethings like us. Sure, some of them had prison records, but who wasn't entitled to a mistake or two? Annabella's owl earrings shook with optimism as she offered to set me up on a double date with her most recent felon's--oh, I'm sorry, boyfriend's--brother. I was noncommittal as I continued to inhale the calamari.

"If it isn't my favorite lawyer!"

"Paul," I said, turning around to face him. "What are you doing here?"

"And it's nice to see you too, Ms. Ryan."

Annabella winked at me and made a hasty retreat to the raw bar serving station. Behind Paul's back, she gave me a thumbs up. Way to stay classy, Annabella.

"Sorry, I didn't mean it like that. I'm, you know, surprised to see you. I guess that means Pamela's here too?"

Paul took the seat next to me. "She is. Does that scare you?"

"Scare me? Will you lose all respect for me if I say yes?"

Paul laughed. "Not at all. She scares me too."

"Why? Did she break your ankle?"

"No. She broke yours?"

"Yes. It's a very long story involving a cheerleading pyramid."

"Sounds fascinating." Paul stood and offered me his hand. "Maybe we both need a drink to deal with this little walk down memory lane."

I took his hand. "Yeah, I think that might help."

We walked past a group of boogying Rosettis and made our way to a bar in the back. I order a glass of pinot grigio, a very lady-like drink I thought. Paul ordered a scotch. Not wanting to revisit my high school humiliation at the hands of Pamela, I asked him if he'd seen a recent Brad Pitt movie. He had, and we chatted about that and other neutral, non-Pamela related topics. Paul, his deep brown eyes never leaving me, was attentive without being overwhelming. If Jim's absence became permanent, Paul wouldn't be a bad transition man. He'd certainly be more acceptable and less scary than Annabella's ex-cons.

While Paul was in the men's room, Deirdre found me. "Did you get a load of that?"

"What?"

"Angela's sleeping with the enemy."

"What do you mean?"

"Look over by the roast pig."

I looked across the crowded Venetian Banquet Room and saw Pamela, resplendent in an aquamarine cocktail dress, laughing with Angela.

"So she invited Pamela. So what? It was probably Elaine's idea anyway."

Deirdre motioned to the bartender. "It doesn't matter to me. I just thought you might care."

"Well, I don't. Not really. Look, we're out, having fun. Certainly more fun than scrapbooking."

"Speak for yourself. I love scrapbooking."

"We're having a nice time anyway. I don't want to fight with Angela, and I don't want to fight with Pamela. We're on the show together, so we might as well get along. In fact, why don't we bite the bullet and go over there and say hello."

"Really?"

"Yes, really. Grab your drink and let's go."

We tottered over in our high heels, my weak left ankle wobbling somewhat. Angela was straightening Pamela's owl pendant when I said, "Hi Pamela. It's nice to see you again. This is my sister, Deirdre. You might remember her. She was a year behind us at Queen of the Rosary."

Not making the same mistake she'd made at the cocktail party, especially with the cameras around, Pamela was charm personified. "Oh yes, Deirdre. Of course. You played tennis, right?"

"That's right."

"And what are you doing now. Are you a lawyer like your sister?"

God, Pamela really knew how to find someone's Achilles heel. It's a gift. Deirdre's always had a chip on her shoulder about not going to a top tier college and people acting like she's *only* a teacher. I knew it hadn't been easy for her to grow up in my academic shadow, just as it hadn't been easy for me to grow up with a petite blond goddess for a sister.

"No, I'm a Special Ed teacher."

"She won an award from New York State last year," I added. She looked like she wanted to strangle me.

"Oh, how impressive," Pamela said.

Deirdre didn't seem to know how to take that, so she said, "Yes, it is rewarding."

"And your husband? Did your sister find you a lawyer to marry?"

Deirdre snapped. "I found my own husband. We went to college together. He's a Physical Education teacher."

"Sounds wonderful."

"Oh, he's a doll, Pammy," Angela added, trying to diffuse the tension. "And he's sooo cute!"

"I'm sure he is." Pamela looked over my shoulder for an escape route. "If you girls will excuse me, I see my husband." Smiling at the camera which had materialized behind us, Pamela sashayed across the floor.

"Well, that went well," I said.

"She is such a bitch," Deirdre fumed. "I feel like breaking her ankle."

"See. I told you."

Angela puffed out her hair. "Oh, you Griffin girls. You're too sensitive. What did she say that was so wrong, other than that your job was impressive?"

"It was the way she said it," Deirdre said.

"Oh, whatever. Anyway, why don't you two try some of the roast pig? I have to go make my speech!" Angela then did her own sashay--after not-so-subtly making sure the cameras were on her--across the Venetian Banquet Room floor.

I looked at the enormous pig's head. "Even I can't face that."

"I'll bet hanging out in the church basement with my cricket doesn't look so bad now."

"I know. I know. But how could I not show up to Angela's party?"

"She's spoken to you a total of ten minutes tonight. The only reason she wanted you here was so she could be on TV. Isn't it obvious?"

"Hello!" Angela screeched in her *Lawn Guyland* voice. "Welcome to Villa Mascaro's. Isn't the food amazing? Thank you Uncle Anthony for hosting the launch party for Angela Rosetti Fine Jewelry. Let's give it up for Anthony Mascaro, everybody!"

Various Mascaros and Rosettis whooped it up, as Angela dragged all five feet, six inches of Uncle Anthony up to the microphone. He looked scared of the cameras, so he just gave a little wave and escaped to the back of the room.

Angela proceeded to thank almost everyone in the room while I succumbed to sampling a slice of the roast pig. It wasn't bad, although after my own little pig-out session, my black skirt felt even tighter than before. I couldn't wait to get home and change into sweats.

"And now, I want to give a special thanks to two of my closest friends from high school. They are both such beautiful and special ladies. And they are both starring in a hot new reality show that my brother Chrissy is working on. Let's give it up for our very own Gold Coast Wives! Come on up here, Pamela Kruger and Kate Ryan!"

I handed my plate of pig to Deirdre and walked up the slippery Venetian Banquet Room floor. Pamela met me half way and startled me by giving me a high five. Since she's about four inches shorter than me, I awkwardly bent down to meet her hand. I heard the slap of our hands and the rip of my skirt at the same time. I froze in horror as Pamela walked ahead of me. She moved Angela out of the way and said into the microphone, "Looks like someone really enjoyed Uncle Anthony's food!"

"Kate always did like eating dinner over at my house. Isn't that right, Kit Kat?"

I quickly made my way to the microphone, now facing the crowd so they couldn't see my fat ass hanging out of the ruined Armani skirt. Deciding to make the best of it, I smiled. "There's nothing like a Mascaro meal. Best of luck, Angela, with your beautiful jewelry."

Chris came up to the microphone and slipped a long jacket over my shoulder, covering the embarrassing tear. Deirdre soon followed and without saying another word to anyone we slipped out of the Venetian Banquet Hall. And my sister only said "I told you so" four times on the way out.

Chapter 7

The morning of the spa day was unseasonably warm for early April--mid-60s with not a cloud in the sky. It was impossible for even me to remain melancholy on such a glorious spring day. Lucy and I walked her doll carriage around the neighborhood. Lucy laughed when a neighbor's cat jumped on the carriage, her deep chuckle so much like Jim's it was heartbreaking.

Marion, Lucy's ex-nanny, arrived at a quarter to twelve. Tina's house was only a ten minute drive away, so I had plenty of time to get there by noon. Lucy ran into Marion's arms the minute she arrived--she had clearly missed her nanny very much. Poor Lucy, her whole world had been turned upside down these past few months.

Tina lived in the Mariners Cliff section of Huntington Bay, a small enclave of craftsman-like cottages hidden among the cliffs overhanging a small cove. Tina's cottage was sparkling white trimmed in a soft baby blue, her small tidy lawn ringed with daffodils.

"Hi. You're early," Tina said in a strong voice. What happened to Marilyn, I wondered.

"It's five after," I said, looking at my watch.

"Oh, I guess you didn't check your email. 'You must check your taping schedule,'" she said in perfect imitation of Harry's Brooklynese.

I laughed and asked whether she wanted me to come back later.

"No, no, it starts at one anyway. Come in. Glass of wine?"

"If I have wine and a massage, I think I'll slip into a coma."

She laughed. Tina had a deep hearty laugh, when she wasn't pretending to be Marilyn Monroe that is. "I just made some fresh lemonade."

"Perfect."

No wonder Elaine had selected Tina's house for the spa day. Tina had knocked out most of the internal walls so that the first floor was one open space. With its bleached oak flooring and floor to ceiling views of the bay, the house was serene and restful.

"Tina, the views are stunning."

"I know, that's what sold me on the place." She handed me a frosty glass of lemonade. "It's too beautiful to be inside, let's sit on the deck." French doors opened up to a redwood deck supported by pilings. Below the deck was a sheer drop of at least twenty feet--good thing I wasn't afraid of heights.

"Tina, if this was my backyard I don't think I would ever leave."

"It gets a little lonely at times on my own. As a weekend home it's perfect. If you follow this path it leads to my dock. I have a small sailboat down there. I'll have to take you and your daughter out sailing someday."

A billy goat couldn't have made it down that path. "Maybe you could pick us up at the yacht club instead," I said, pointing to the treacherous path.

Tina smiled. "I could do that."

We spent the next forty minutes or so chatting about Tina's travels to India, her childhood in South Carolina, her recent off-off-Broadway auditions. We talked about everything other than *Gold Coast Wives*. I think Tina realized I was making it through the taping schedule by the skin of my teeth. Tom and crew soon arrived, disturbing the bubble of intimacy that had arisen between us.

"Here we go again," I moaned. "Don't the cameras and the lighting and all that rigmarole ever get to you?"

She laughed. "I grew up on camera." Tina opened the French doors and said in a breathy Marilyn Monroe voice, "Hi, Tom. Can I get you a drink?"

I sipped my lemonade and enjoyed the spring sun. Tom and crew set up, and the other two Wives arrived. Fifteen minutes later Tina came out and said, "Kate, we're ready to start filming. Can you go back to your car and drive around the block. They want to film the entrance."

"But that's stupid. I'm already here!"

Tina gave me a blank look, her Marilyn persona now in place. I shrugged my shoulders and followed her through the French doors.

Rachel's and Pamela's *entrances* were filmed first, so it looked like I was the last to arrive. Tina, in a skimpy pink leotard, opened the front door and said with enough enthusiasm worthy of another Emmy, "Kate! You made it!"

I couldn't restrain myself from rolling my eyes. "Yes, of course I'm here."

"Welcome. Come in. The other girls are waiting." Rachel and Pamela sprawled on the bleached cotton couches, sipping white wine and wearing colorful and revealing leotards. I was wearing black sweatpants and a white t-shirt, as per Tom's instructions.

"Kate, so glad you could finally join us," Pamela said in a voice that, had she not spent four year torturing me in high school, I would've thought was sincere.

"Hello, Pamela. Hi, Rachel."

"Hello," Rachel said with venom.

"Girls," Tina said, "before we have our massages, why don't we warm up with some yoga. You're all familiar with the sun salutation?" Sun salu-what?

"I love the sun salutation," Pamela said as she laid out her purple yoga mat. Rachel and Tina followed suit with their yoga mats. Of course, I had no mat.

Tina contorted her long limbs into what I assumed was a yoga pose as Rachel and Pamela easily followed her lead. I just stood there.

"You don't know yoga, Kate?" Pamela asked as she was doing something called the plank pose.

"No." I'd tried yoga once a few years ago when Fowler Sherman had enacted a short lived work-life balance summit after yet another forty-something lawyer had suffered a heart attack. Apparently sitting in front of a computer screen for thirteen hours a day while inhaling donuts was an unhealthy lifestyle. The summit had been discontinued once HR had noticed a drop in billables, conducted a cost-benefit analysis and determined that after the yoga classes had been introduced, there were more Fowler Sherman lawyers missing work to visit their chiropractors than there were heart attack victims.

"Kate," said Tina, "why don't you start with downward dog. It will help you open up your chakras and make the massage more effective."

"My chakras are fine, thanks. I'll just watch."

"It's easy," Tina said in her breathy voice, "I'll help you. Bend over."

At this point the cameras were on me, so I felt I had no choice but to attempt the downward dog. I placed my hands on the floor and stuck my ass in the air, and had started to feel a nice stretch when a hand pushed my back down toward the floor.

"Your posture is all wrong," Pamela said as she continued *helping me*.

I heard the crack before I actually felt it and then let out a bloodcurdling scream. Two production assistants quickly lifted me to the couch, while another went to get a bag of ice. I was in so much pain I couldn't even cry.

Without missing a beat, the Wives continued their yoga moves. I guess the show must go on. I tried to stifle my moans, whimpering softly so as not to disturb them.

After a half hour, the Wives were sufficiently limber and the stabbing pain in my back became a less painful throbbing, so we were ready to start our massages. Tom helped me stagger up the stairs to the massage table set up for me in one of Tina's guest rooms while the other Wives went to their respective tables downstairs.

I stripped down to my underwear and slid under the massage table's crisp white sheets. My masseuse was a blond surfer dude, I'd say early to mid-thirties. New-agey music played on the house-wide speakers. I dozed as surfer dude massaged my damaged lower back. After twenty minutes I flipped over onto my back and dozed again as he massaged my feet. I dreamed about Jim walking on a beach with me. His hair was blowing in the wind as he nibbled on my ear. I felt Jim caress my breasts. I gave a small moan and then opened my left eye. This wasn't a dream. Surfer dude was giving me a breast massage.

"How does that feel? Your muscles are really tight," he said, not stopping the strange circular movements.

"I think I'm fine. I've had enough massage." I tried to sit up, but the sharp pain in my lower back immobilized me.

"I'm not finished," surfer dude said as he continued to pummel my breasts.

"Yes. You are."

"Okay, can I get you some water?" he asked in his professional, solicitous, surfer dude voice.

"I'm fine, thanks." I attempted to roll over onto my side.

"Don't get up too quickly and make sure you drink plenty of water today, it will help flush out all the toxins." The breast toxins?

I laid there a few minutes, trying to work up the energy to stand. I didn't know about the breast massage, but surfer dude did help my back. The pain was still there, but it wasn't as unbearable as before. I could hear the murmur of the Wives chatting downstairs. I wondered if they'd enjoyed their breast massages.

I was able to stand, only slightly bent, and put on the white cotton robe Mr. Breast Massage had left for me. As I crept down the stairs, I heard Pamela say, "... she really has some nerve. Not only did she arrive late to my book launch and leave early, all she did was throw herself at Don's brother-in-law while she was there. It was embarrassing, really. I can't imagine that he would ever have any interest in her. And isn't she still married? Typical. But, I'm not surprised. She did the same thing in high school, threw herself at any guy who looked at her." Guys? What guys? It was an all-girls school. "Believe me, she had quite the reputation in high school." What reputation? As a math nerd?

"I know what you mean, Pamela. She was constantly fawning over my staff when we so graciously decorated her great room. For free, I might add," Rachel said. Does offering Garrett a tissue after Rachel made him cry constitute fawning? Okay, I guess I had been fawning. "Not that she was grateful," Rachel continued. "Not that she ever even said thank you."

"And to just waltz in here, after keeping us waiting twenty minutes. It's rude. So disrespectful of everyone else's time. If that's the way she acts it's no wonder she got fired," Pamela said. "I can't believe you didn't say anything to her, Tina."

"Would you like another drink?" Tina asked. Tina was clearly Switzerland.

"What I'd like is to finish up this spa day. I have a book signing in Garden City at five. Of course I assume we have to wait for her."

"What the hell is she doing?" Rachel asked. "Probably shtupping the massage therapist."

"Figures she's the only one who got a male masseuse," Pamela said, laughing. "She probably attacked him."

This was too much. I didn't mind so much when the Wives ignored me or excluded me, but to tell these outright lies, on camera no less. I didn't sign on for this. I crept back to my room and with effort changed into my sweats. I made my way down the back staircase without detection, opened the front door and was almost at my car when I heard Elaine say, "Forget something, Kate?"

"No, I'm leaving. I've had enough."

"We're not finished filming," Elaine said without her usual manic smile.

"Well, I'm finished!"

"Get back in there, Kate. Your contract obligates you to two more complete tapings. This taping isn't complete."

"So sue me!"

"Don't think I won't," she said, now within inches from my face. "And then you'll have to return your stipend and be liable to Channel 45 for damages." She gave me a triumphant smile. "You're not the only one who can read a contract."

"Fine," I said turning around.

I walked in the front door to hear Rachel laughing while Pamela said, "... and the teachers had to clear the gym to make way for the paramedics."

"Hi, girls," I interrupted. "Did you enjoy your massages?" I asked with a bright, fake smile. "Mine was just sooo relaxing. That Brad has magic hands."

"I'll bet," Rachel snorted.

"Oh, he most certainly did. It was the most satisfying massage I've had in quite some time," I purred. If I was going to be painted with the slut brush, I might as well have some fun with it. "I really worked up an appetite!"

"My chef made a delightful, healthy lunch. Fillet of sole with an organic garden salad. Let me see if it's ready." Tina escaped to the kitchen.

"Sounds delicious, doesn't it Pamela?" I asked, forcing her to talk to me.

"Yes it does," Pamela replied.

"Oh, Pamela," I said, "I'm sorry I left early the other evening, but I do believe I told you I had another engagement."

"You left early?" Pamela said, "I didn't even notice."

"I wanted to apologize anyway," I said with a saccharine smile. Pamela said nothing, but she exchanged a look with Rachel.

"Oh, Rachel, how did the photos of the great room turn out?" I asked with fake enthusiasm. "Will you be able to use them for your spring ads?"

"I don't know," Rachel said. "David is in charge of the advertising."

"Oh, I thought that was why you insisted we finish it last week, so we would meet your advertisers' deadline."

"I wanted everything to be done before your husband came home," Rachel said with an evil glint. "When is he due home again?"

"I believe next week. It's a shame he's going to miss the ball," I said, trying to look disappointed.

Tina walked in from the kitchen and looked at us with concern--I guess she didn't want any bloodshed on her white couches.

"Lunch is ready. We're eating on the deck, this way." Tina led us through the French doors.

"Oh great!" I enthused. "I'm starving! Aren't you starving, Rachel?" Rachel probably hadn't felt hunger since 1978.

Now all I had to do was get through lunch without pitching Rachel or Pamela off the deck.

Easier said than done.

Chapter 8

The next afternoon, Chris and Angela were in stitches as I described my breast massage.

"Maybe you shouldn't have stopped him," Angela said.

"Oh please, with my luck, Tom and crew would've picked that moment to film it. It's bad enough Pamela has made me out to be the slut of Queen of the Rosary!"

"That is just too funny," Angela said with a laugh. "You, of all people!"

"Okay, you're done." Chris sprayed Angela's elaborate hairstyle. "Can I trust you to do your own make up?"

"Of course," Angela huffed.

"Remember, Angela, less is more. Now you," Chris said turning to me. "How do you want your hair?"

"Down?"

"Yes, I think down is better. It covers those unfortunate ears. Over to the sink," he commanded.

Twenty minutes later, Chris had arranged my hair in a halo of soft curls, with my ears camouflaged. "There is no way I'm touching your makeup, my delicate little flower. I suggest you go with this dark red lipstick. Now where is that sister of yours? I'm due at Pamela's in less than an hour."

"Well, we wouldn't want to keep Pamela waiting."

"Honestly, Kate," Chris said, as he blasted my hair with a final shot of his industrial strength hair spray, "I know she gives you a hard time, but she's not that bad. Believe me, I've seen worse."

"Why do you think she's mean to me? I've never understood why she hated me so much. Look, I know I was a little nerdy in high school," I admitted.

"A lot nerdy," Angela chirped from the bathroom.

"Okay, a lot nerdy. But Queen of the Rosary was chock full of nerds. Why didn't she just ignore me? I know Angela thinks I harp on this, but she deliberately threw me off that pyramid."

Chris checked the back of my hair one more time. "Kate, if you were such a nerd, how did you even make it onto the cheerleading team in the first place?"

"Blame your sister. I was quite happy in my drama club-slash-school newspaper world. Angie's the one who convinced the coach to let me on the team after one of the cheerleaders transferred to public school."

"Obviously I've been around women a lot since I became a stylist, and I've heard many variations of the mean girl scenario. I think it usually stems from some type of jealousy."

"Pamela jealous of me? Why?"

"Oh, Kate," Chris said, "stop fishing for compliments. You're funny, you're smart. I have to imagine you had a lot of friends in high school. Wasn't Pamela also friends with Angela? Maybe Pamela was jealous of your friendship? Maybe she was jealous of your good grades?"

"Okay, even if all of that was true, why is she being nasty to me now? She looks fantastic, she's living on an estate in Lloyd Neck and she's married to a multi-millionaire. Hell, she's even a published author. She's the big success story. How am I a threat to her?"

"I think there's trouble brewing in paradise. Whenever I'm there, her husband doesn't even look at her. As far as I can tell, she has no real friends other than Rachel, and she only met her a few weeks ago. I kind of feel sorry for her."

"Sorry for Pamela Reynolds? Please."

"Well, feel sorry for me if I'm late," Chris said. "Now, where is your sister?"

"We're here, we're here," Dee said, racing through the door with her gorgeous husband. "Sorry I'm late! That frickin' Wii, I swear I'm throwing it in the garbage!"

"Quick, Deirdre, get over to the sink. Gordon, I think you need a trim," Chris said.

"I do?"

"Yes, take off your jacket, and I'll give you a trim after I'm done with your wife."

Within thirty minutes, Chris had arranged Deirdre's curls in a messy, almost-Grecian updo that perfectly complimented the toga-inspired cream silk gown she'd found on sale at Macy's--she looked like a petite blond goddess. Gordon's blond locks were trimmed--and dressed in a rented tuxedo, he'd give Brad Pitt a run for his money.

Angela was the real surprise of the evening. With her makeup subdued and her curves clothed in a simple dark blue gown, she looked like an Italian Audrey Hepburn.

"You all look gorgeous," Chris said, which must have been true because he almost never gave compliments. "The limo will be here around seven. I'll see you later."

We still had another forty five minutes to kill before the limo was due, so Gordon opened the box of twelve bottles of complementary champagne Channel 45 had sent over the night before. We drank a glass in my new great room, where Angela admired the crystal lion. Jerry, togged out in a new purchased and obviously uncomfortable Armani tux, arrived and joined us for another glass of champagne. Since I was in my robe and still stiff from my yoga attempt, Angela and Dee joined me in my bedroom to help me put on my new blood-red floor length gown. I normally never wore red, but Chris had convinced me that the old redheads-can't-wear-red rule was passe.

I winced as I raised my arms and Dee pulled the gown over my head.

"Does the back still hurt, Kate?" Dee asked with concern.

"Not as bad as yesterday, but it's still very, very stiff. So long as I don't move too much, I should be fine."

"How are you going to get through the evening without moving?" Dee opened her purse. "Here take this," she said, handing me a blue, horse-sized pill.

"What is it?"

"It's just a muscle relaxant. It's nothing. Take it. It will make your back feel better,"

Normally I don't take anything stronger than aspirin, and I certainly never avail myself of any of Dee's magic pills. I don't even ask her where she gets them--it must be some type of suburban teacher prescription drug network. However it was clear a night in heels was only going to make my back feel worse. Plus, I was lurching around like Frankenstein, so my posture didn't do justice to the designer duds. Hoping for the best, I washed the horse pill down with Angela's glass of champagne.

After I slipped on the matching red stilettos, we joined the boys in the great room and finished another bottle of champagne. We felt quite merry by the time the limo arrived yet managed to polish off another bottle during our twenty minute drive to Oheka Castle. Giggly from the champagne, we spilled out of the limo in all our finery and clambered up the stone steps with two Channel 45 cameras in tow.

Almost a century old, Oheka Castle was built on the highest point on Long Island during the Gold Coast's Gilded Age and is blessed with magnificent views of Cold Spring Harbor. According to the sign we read on the way in, it is the second largest private residence ever built in the United States and includes over one hundred thousand square feet and one hundred twenty-seven rooms. Its original owner, financier Otto Kahn, had regularly entertained royalty, heads of state and Hollywood stars. He must have been rolling over in his grave at the thought of his former home being overrun by overdressed, high strung cat fanciers.

Garrett was manning the welcome table in front of the Grand Ballroom and organizing the raffle tickets when we made our tipsy entrance. He looked up and snapped, "Kate, you're late. Rachel has been looking all over for you."

"Oh for God's sake, I can't be late. The ball doesn't start until eight."

"Rachel expected you to arrive early and help arrange the sponsors' signage and set out the red carpet for the photographers. She's on the war path." Garrett seemed happy that Rachel's rage was directed at someone else for a change.

"Tom," I said, grabbing his sleeve as he walked past, "did you or did you not tell me to get here by seven-thirty? It's only seven-twenty now."

"I don't recall. Sorry, there's a lighting crisis I have to take care of." And with that he scurried down the hall like the weasel he was.

"I am sick of them telling me I'm late all the time," I huffed, losing my buzz.

"Oh, who cares," Deirdre said. "We're out without children, there's free booze and music."

"And food, Kit Kat," Angela said. "Chris told me they're having a Viennese Hour, like at my wedding. How can you be sad when there are unlimited pastries? Come on, relax. Let's just have fun tonight."

"You're right," I conceded. "Only another few more hours, and I'll be a retired Gold Coast Wife anyway, so let's hit the bar!"

"Not before we hit the red carpet. Girls, make sure your owls are straight!" Angela dragged us to the *red carpet*, which consisted of two bored photographers in a small hallway hung with signs from the very impressive sponsors of the LICKs Ball. The most prominent signs were from Petatopia and the Suffolk County Humane Society. The photographers perked up when they saw our cleavage. Angela was shameless as she flirted with the short, balding photographer and made him take a close up of our owl pendants. I think he was happy to have an excuse to take some boob shots.

With our owl promotion duties complete, we toddled in our high heels to join the boys at the bar. Since the bartender wasn't there yet, Jerry jumped behind the bar and made us dirty martinis. The band warmed up with *Ain't Too Proud to Beg*, and Gordon and Deirdre danced. I was laughing at Jerry's impression of the flamboyant lead singer when someone tapped me on the shoulder.

"Oh, Kate, I'm so glad you could finally make it," Rachel said, oozing sarcasm.

"The limo that Channel 45 arranged picked me up at seven. I am right on time."

"Right on time?" she shouted. "You promised to help me set up. Don't you remember?"

"How could I remember? You haven't spoken a civil word to me in weeks."

"When I was in your kitchen I specifically remember you agreed to help me set up. But, I guess that was before you got thirty thousand dollars of free furniture off me!" Rachel screeched. She was beginning to hurt my ears. However, since she said it, I did vaguely remember agreeing to help. But she'd never followed up. Besides, wasn't the production crew supposed to coordinate all this LICKS Ball nonsense anyway? Notwithstanding my rationalizations, I started to feel a little guilty, so I said in a more conciliatory tone, "Rachel, I'm sorry if there was a mix-up. Is there anything you'd like me to help you with now?"

"Now? After you've clearly been drinking? I don't think so. This is my night," she started to wail. "This is my charity! My charity! I'm not letting a bunch of lousy Irish drunks ruin it for me! David! David! I need you!" She then stomped off in search of the ever-patient David. I looked over and saw that Tom and crew had caught Rachel's meltdown on tape. Tom looked shell-shocked. I think he'd half-expected me to punch her.

"Doesn't that bitch realize we're Italian?" Angela said to Jerry.

"I guess you and Jerry are Irish drunks by association," I said.

"Good thing Grace and Johnny aren't here," Dee said, laughing, "Grace would've laid her out!"

"Ah, forget about it. She's a nut." Jerry gave me a little hug. "Who needs another martini?"

The ballroom filled up. After I recovered from Rachel's ethnic slur, I started to relax and enjoy sipping Jerry's martinis and listening to imitations of Angela's design-process. Angela periodically hit him over the head with her silky evening bag. I tried not to notice Rachel scurrying around with a clipboard, followed by Garrett and the other poor souls she'd recruited from Finley's Fine Furnishings. Rachel was so frantic that even her new best friend Pamela avoided her.

For a minute I contemplated walking across the dance floor to greet Pamela and Don, but I was having fun where I was and not quite sure I was up for any more abuse.

The muscle relaxant had begun to work its magic, and I was swaying to the music without any stiffness or pain.

"We meet again."

I looked up and smiled at Paul Goodman, my grizzly friend.

"Don't tell me that Pamela roped you into attending another one of these things."

"I've always been very concerned about the plight of the suburban cat."

"I know, sometimes the thought of all those little kitties wandering around without their kibble…it just makes me want to cry."

"I'm sure it does," he said with a chuckle. "Hey, would you like to walk over to the silent auction table and help me pick something to bid on? I promised Don I'd spend a lot of money tonight."

"Sure. Everyone I came with seems to think they're on *Dance Fever*."

"Oh, would you prefer to dance?" Paul asked.

"Absolutely not!" I said. Paul looked a bit taken aback. "Not that I wouldn't like to dance with you, but I don't dance. With anyone. I'm a terrible dancer."

"Oh, I'm sure you're just being modest. You probably don't think a Hoosier like me can dance."

"Paul, I'm a Long Island gal. I'm not even exactly sure what a Hoosier is."

Paul laughed. "Let's go over and waste some money before I feel the need to give you a lecture on the history of the Hoosiers and the fine State of Indiana." Paul placed his hand on my bare back and gently guided me through the crowded ballroom. It was such a casual yet intimate gesture. It had been so long since I'd been touched by a man in that way that I became somewhat flustered. I could feel my cheeks flame.

As we weaved our way through the ballroom, I tried to figure out the crowd. Similar to Pamela's book launch party, there was a heavy contingent of Don's business associates along with Pamela's North Shore socialite acquaintances. Rachel had clearly recruited a large number of supporters, recognizable by their braying voices and heavy jewelry. Channel 45 managed to fill several tables with a mix of production executives in ill-fitting tuxedos, sprinkled with the Channel 45 on-air talent. I recognized Carolyn Cramer, the well preserved fifty-year-old news anchor of *Long Island Today*, and Miss Kippy from *Reading with Miss Kippy*, the show I forced Lucy to watch on occasion when I felt she was on Dora overload. Tina, surrounded by at least ten handsome actor-slash-model types all under the age of twenty-five, gave me a sly smile as we walked past.

The silent auction items ranged from a haircut at a local salon to a weekend at a bed and breakfast on the North Fork, Long Island's wine country. Lucy's birthday was coming up, so I bid on a children's party package consisting of a clown and a snow white princess. Don bid on several items: the weekend on the North Fork, a dinner for two at Le Cirque and a package of tickets to various Broadway shows.

"Wow," I said, "those auction items look great. You're going to make some lady happy."

He looked at me for a moment and then said, "I hope so."

I was confused. Did that mean he had a girlfriend? Did that mean he wanted to take me out? Even at my dating prime I hadn't been the best at reading men's flirting signals, and after ten years of being off the market, I was completely clueless. In order to fill the uncomfortable silence, I began to babble on about Lucy's birthday party, clowns and my sister's irrational fear of them when, thank God, I was interrupted by the microphone's loud screech. A small stage had been set up to the left of the silent auction area, near the front of the ballroom. Behind the stage a large banner read LICKs 2009. Rachel was haranguing one of the Channel 45 technicians as the microphone continued its high piercing scream. Finally, before our eardrums started to bleed, the technical difficulties were solved, and Rachel's voice boomed across the ballroom.

"Welcome," she began. "Welcome to the first annual LICKs Ball!"

There was a decent amount of applause. I looked over at Dee and Gordon and could see that, once again, Dee was laughing over the event's name. I swear, sometimes she was worse than the thirteen year old boys she taught.

"Long Island Cats and Kittens launched a little over six months ago and in that short period of time has become the number one feline rescue organization on Long Island." Rachel waited for more applause. After a few moments she was rewarded with a feeble smattering of clapping. Undeterred, she described in excruciating detail the amazing strides LICKs had made during its short life. Paul asked if he could get me another drink and despite the fact that I was beyond the tipsy stage,

I agreed. Rachel had finished her history of the cat when she began to thank the various sponsors of the event. I started to zone out when I heard Rachel thank the chairpeople.

"... and I want to give a special thanks to my fellow Gold Coast Wives who have worked tirelessly over the past several weeks to make the LICKs Ball a success. Pamela Kruger and Tina Andrews, please come up here. I have a special gift for you."

Suddenly there was a Channel 45 camera in my face, looking for my reaction at being excluded. I smiled and clapped while trying not to look at the camera.

Paul appeared and handed me a flute of champagne. With a gallant smile, he looked straight at the camera. "I want to toast the most beautiful Gold Coast Wife, Kate Ryan." He tapped his glass against mine and kissed me on the cheek.

I gave Paul a grateful smile. Several people around us looked in our direction, and I caught Pamela staring at us from the stage.

Rachel finished her thank you's and announced the buffet was open.

"Paul, I've been drinking champagne since six this evening. I think I'd better have something to eat before I start dancing on the tables."

"I thought you didn't dance."

"I never dance *willingly*. However, it has been known to happen after a few too many cocktails. And believe me, it's not pretty."

"Okay, much as I'd love to see it, I'm hungry too. Let's go." Paul once again guided me through the crowd with his strong hand on my bare back.

Typical fare at these things consisted of an assortment of rubber chicken and indeterminate beef dishes. However, Oheka was known for its food and Rachel had selected the premium package. I hadn't eaten since breakfast. I loaded up at the various carving stations, with an assortment of prime rib, sushi and vegetarian lasagna. Paul eyed my plate.

"Are you really going to eat all that?"

"You better believe it. And I'll probably go back for seconds." He might as well know up front, a delicate eater I was not.

Paul's table was closest to the buffet and since my crowd was still indulging their inner disco queens, Paul and I sat at his table. Pamela was circling the ballroom bestowing air kisses on everyone in her path, so I didn't think she'd be heading back to the table anytime soon. As we ate dinner, Paul and I chatted with Don's CFO and his young wife. The food, along with a large glass of water, sobered me up enough to have control of myself but not lose my happy buzz. It was the last night of my *Gold Coast Wives* indentured servitude, I was wearing a dress that flattered both my coloring and my figure--no mean task--and, more importantly, I was being fawned over by an intelligent, funny, attractive man who, at least for a few hours, had made me forget my status as an abandoned wife. Life was good.

As I finished up my second plate, Don joined us at the table with a large, heaping plate of prime rib.

"Hey, Donny," Paul said. "What are you doing with red meat? I thought Pamela told me the other night you all were vegetarians now."

"I'm a vegetarian in Lloyd Neck. Everywhere else I'm an unapologetic carnivore," he said, giving me an *aren't I a naughty boy* wink.

I nervously looked around to see if Pamela was in the vicinity. I was having a good time and didn't want to give her the opportunity to insult me in front of my new boyfriend, or rather, in front of Paul. I caught sight of her ruffled burgundy evening gown on the other side of the ballroom-- it looked like I was safe for the moment.

"Kate," Don said in between mouthfuls of the verboten prime rib, "are you disappointed the show is over?"

"Disappointed? You've got to be kidding. I'm counting the hours until it's over. For your information," I said looking at my watch, "I only have fifty five minutes until my contracted *Gold Coast Wives* duties will be done forever."

"Really? Pamela is sad to see it end. I don't know what she'll do with herself now." Oh, I don't know, pull the wings off flies? Torture puppies, perhaps? I was sure she'd think of something. "Not me," is all I said.

"That's funny. Why did you agree to do the show, if you don't mind me asking?"

"All I can say, Don, is that it seemed like a good idea at the time."

"Yeah, I know what you mean," Don said with a pensive look. I had a feeling he wasn't talking about the show anymore. He took a sip of wine and then turned to me and asked, "Will you be speaking at the New York Asset Managers Symposium next month?"

"I'm not speaking this year, no. I will be attending, though. Will you?"

"Oh, yes, I try not to miss it. Paul, are you coming?"

"I wouldn't miss it."

"Paul, I'm sorry. I never even asked what you do. Do you work with Don?" I said, feeling a little stupid.

"We were too busy talking about your dancing skills to discuss careers," he said, laughing. "I've worked with Don almost ten years, isn't that right, Donny?"

"Yeah, about that," Don said. "Til he abandoned me."

"Not 'abandoned,' Don, 'branched out.' I was the head of DTK's marketing up until two years ago when I started my own consulting firm. I advise large endowments and pension funds regarding their allocations to alternative investments, such as hedge funds."

"I suppose at some point everyone has to be his own man, his own boss. Can't fault you for that." Don shoveled more prime rib into his mouth. The man was acting like he hadn't been fed in days. "This is great. Reminds me of the Sunday dinners Suzanne used to make, doesn't it, Paul?"

The joking twinkle that had been in Paul's eyes all evening was suddenly subdued, and he quietly replied, "It sure does, Donny."

"I swear, no one could cook like my Suzy. Remember her leg of lamb?" Don asked. I think it was more than the red meat he missed.

"Well, isn't this cozy," I heard behind me. Oh no. I was so caught up in the conversation that I had lost track of Pamela. "Darling," Pamela purred, "I can't believe you started dinner without me."

"I didn't know you were eating tonight," Don said, his expression blank.

"Oh, for goodness sake, Don," Pamela fake scolded, "why wouldn't I eat dinner?"

"You should try the prime rib, Pamela," Paul said. "It's delicious."

"Oh, I think I'll just have some pasta. We don't eat red meat anymore, right, Don?"

Don didn't answer, and since he had cleared his plate, the evidence gone. I was thinking about how to escape, in a way that didn't look like Pamela had scared me off, when I felt someone grab my arm.

"Come on, Kate, you have to dance to this one!" Deirdre dragged me to my feet. The band had started to play *I Will Survive*. Sit here with Pamela or dance to a Gloria Gaynor song in front of my new pseudo-boyfriend? Tough choice, but this time Gloria won. I smiled at Paul, allowing myself to be carried off by Dee.

Gloria must've been a fan favorite of the Channel 45 execs because they were all on the floor, cummerbunds askew. The dance floor was crowded and we couldn't move much, keeping my awkward lurching dance moves to a minimum. Angela's elaborate updo was beginning to come loose as she sang, or rather shouted, every word of the song. For a woman who'd never been dumped, she sure seemed to like this song.

The band segued into *It's Raining Men*, which seemed to be yet another favorite of the Channel 45 execs. Tina and three of her underage admirers joined our dance circle and at one point I was doing the bump with one of the little fellas. When the band began to play *YMCA*, the girls were finally discoed out. We snaked our way through the crowd and found a spot at the bar where the bartender poured us glasses of champagne. As we caught our breath and gossiped about the crowd, Deirdre scanned the room looking for Gordon.

"Where do you think the boys are, Angela?"

"Oh, Jerry ran into one of his clients. I can see him on the patio smoking a cigar." Angela pointed to the large glass doors leading out to one of the elaborate gardens.

"Is Gordon with him? I don't see him."

"Oh, relax," Angela said, "I'm sure he'll turn up. Maybe he's in the men's room."

When the band began to play one of those indeterminate slow songs that sounded familiar, I felt a hand on my shoulder.

"May I have this dance?" Paul asked.

"Oh, I don't dance."

He took my hand and led me to the dance floor. "Then what was it I just saw you doing?"

"I'm not sure that could be classified as dancing," I said as the girls giggled. "Okay, I give up. Don't say I didn't warn you."

With a calm assurance that I found sexy, Paul took my right hand and placed his other hand on my lower back. As he led me around the dance floor. I cleared my mind and concentrated on following his lead. Soon, we were gliding around the floor, and I could feel several eyes, and cameras, following us. I stumbled, but Paul's strong lead carried me along. Our movements became effortless and mid-way through the song I looked up into his dark brown eyes.

"This isn't so bad," I admitted.

Paul pulled me closer and murmured, "Not bad at all."

The song melted into another slow song medley, and we continued to circle the enormous dance floor. I caught sight of our reflection in the glass doors lining the east side of the ballroom and couldn't believe that the tall, elegant and--dare I say it--beautiful woman dancing so well with the broad shouldered man was really me. For the first time in months, all my worries and insecurities melted away as I focused on the movement and warmth between myself and this alluring stranger.

Paul and I had begun our final circle around the dance floor when I heard a familiar voice rise above the music.

"Get off him, you little whore!"

I abruptly stopped dancing. "I think that was my sister. I'd better see what's going on."

"Of course," Paul replied.

We walked toward the shouting, and I could see Deirdre grab the arm of a beautiful dark-haired girl dressed in a microscopic pink mini dress. The girl, who couldn't have been more than twenty, was almost a half foot taller than Dee. I was surprised my petite sister had the strength to pull her off Gordon.

Before we reached them I saw a flash of burgundy ruffle and heard Pamela shout, "What on earth are you doing to my niece!"

"I should have known this slut was related to you! Tell her to go back to trawling the fraternity parties and to keep her hands off my husband."

"Deirdre, please," begged Gordon as he held her arm.

"And you," Deirdre said turning to Gordon. "Get your hands off me and wipe that lipstick off your cheek!"

"Deirdre," I said. "Let's go. Let's get our coats and go."

"Yes," said Pamela, "I think that's an excellent idea."

"Shut up, Pamela," I snapped. "We already said we're leaving. And you," I said looking at the crying niece, "keep your hands, and your lips, off other people's husbands."

"Please," Pamela sneered, "who are you? The morality police? Where's your husband?"

"You're ruining my event!" Rachel wailed as she and David rushed in. "Get out, Kate Ryan. You and your drunk hooligan family. Just get out!"

I looked at my watch and then looked over at Elaine, who was watching the scene from the sidelines. "I have twenty more minutes left on my contracted appearance time, Elaine. Am I allowed to leave now without violating my contract?"

"Yes," Elaine said without any discernible inflection. "Just go."

"Fine. Ladies," I said looking at Rachel and Pamela, "it's been a pleasure. Come on, Dee, let's get out of here."

Angela and Jerry were out on the patio with Jerry's clients and had missed the spectacle. I gave them the abridged version and told them we were leaving. I grabbed Deirdre and Gordon and started heading out the door when I saw Paul.

"Weren't you going to say goodbye?" Paul asked with a small smile.

"Paul, I loved our dance, and I'm sorry I have to leave so, so abruptly."

"I understand."

And with a small wave to Paul, I left the ballroom and my life as a Gold Coast Wife.

Chapter 9

The next morning I woke to the sound of rain pelting the windows and the smell of coffee and bacon. Deirdre had been absolutely wasted last night. I was surprised she had risen before me--and had cooked breakfast no less. I shuffled into the bathroom and inspected the damage. Fortunately, I had washed off my makeup and slathered on night cream last night, so the face didn't look too bad. The soft waves Chris had created yesterday were glued to my head. I decided to hop in the shower before heading down to face my sister.

After my hot shower, I encased my sore body--the muscle relaxants having worn off--in a soft sweat suit. I limped my way downstairs and was surprised to see my mother sitting at the kitchen table, tapping away on her Mac.

"Good morning!" Grace chirped. "Your breakfast is in the warming drawer."

I yawned. "How'd you get here, Mom?"

"I didn't want to wake your father, so I drove myself," she preened. "I took the side streets though. You know how I don't like the expressway."

"Why are you here so early?"

"Early? It's past eleven. To tell you the truth," she said in a lower voice, "I didn't want to be at Deirdre's when Gordon woke up. I assumed something had happened when she didn't come home with Gordon last night. Besides, I had to drop off her ladyship to you anyway."

"How was Lucy? She didn't give you too much trouble last night, did she?"

"Not a bit. She ate her dinner, although she did try and monopolize that blasted Wii. But Lindsay and Brendan were very good and let her have it most of the time."

"Oh, great." I dug into my scrambled eggs.

"How was last night?" Mom asked.

"You know what, Ma, I can't tell you on an empty stomach. Why don't you tell me about your book?"

"I'm on page two hundred already, if you can believe it," my mother said, always happy to turn to her favorite subject. "The words are pouring out of me. I'm glad you suggested this, Kate, and if *On the Shores of the Shannon* is ever published, I'm going to dedicate it to you."

"What about me?" Deirdre said as she dragged herself into the kitchen.

"Didn't I dedicate *Over the Hills and Far Away* to you, and I don't think you ever read it!"

"Ow! Don't shout, Mom," Deirdre begged. "My head can't take it."

"Here." I handed her a mug of coffee. "Sit down, and I'll bring you your breakfast."

"That I cooked," Grace added.

"Yes, that Mom cooked."

"And some Advil, please," my poor sister croaked.

I found the Advil bottle in Deirdre's bag and handed her three tablets, keeping two for myself.

"The pair of you," Grace said, shaking her head. "I swear you'll be the death of me yet. Now tell me already, what happened last night?"

"Do you want me to go first?" I asked, looking at Deirdre. My sister nodded as she swallowed her Advil.

"As you know, we all met here first, and Chris did our hair. Channel 45 sent over some champagne, and we had drinks before the limo picked us up."

"Oh, a limo!" My mother tends to be easily impressed.

"Yes, Channel 45 went all out. Anyway, the limo dropped us off at Oheka Castle. You remember that place, right, Mom? Uncle Bobby's daughter Dawn had her wedding there."

"How fancy," Grace cooed.

"Then Rachel, the one who did the great room, well she was pissed that I wasn't there early to help set up. She went completely off the rails and called us all a bunch of drunks."

"A bunch of Irish drunks," Deirdre added.

"She did not! The bloody cow!"

"She did. And we weren't even really drunk at that point either. At first, things went well. We danced and the food was great, although we missed the Viennese Hour. I was dancing with this nice man Paul, I think I told you I had met him at another *Gold Coast Wives* event, and then I heard Dee shouting."

"Shouting?" my mother asked, appalled. "In public?"

"It was Gordon's fault," Deirdre grumbled, "and Pamela Reynolds' slut of a niece."

"What happened, Dee? What got you upset? I was dancing with Paul, so I didn't see."

"They played a slow dance, and you were off with your boyfriend." With that, my mother's eyes nearly fell out of her head. "And Angela was with Jerry on the patio. I was standing there on my own. I figured Gordon was in the men's room or getting a drink, but one song turned into two and still no Gordon." Deirdre took a sip of her coffee. "I was standing there alone like an idiot, watching everyone else dance. I saw you dancing, Katie, and I couldn't believe it. Mom, you'd have been shocked. She was good and didn't trip once. That Paul can really move too."

"Did you think so?" I asked, quite pleased, compliments on my dancing being few and far between. "Wait, enough about me. When did you see Gordon and the slut?"

"Relax, I'm getting to it. Anyway, I was watching you and Paul, and I noticed his hand went a little too far south, if you know what I mean. Not that I saw you complaining." Again, my mother, for all of her get-on-with-your-life talk, looked a bit shocked. "I caught sight of the back of Gordon's head," Deirdre continued, "and it looked like he was dancing with someone. Which was fine. We've been married eighteen years, he's allowed to dance with someone else. I'm not a complete lunatic."

"Of course not," I agreed.

"I walked closer to see who he was dancing with, and I saw it was a young girl. Again, not a big deal. But then, the little bitch looked straight at me and deliberately started nibbling on Gordon's ear. The brazen hussy kissed his cheek, all the while giving me this satisfied grin. In fairness to Gordon, he seemed pretty surprised and took a step back. I couldn't believe that snotty little bitch had the nerve to do that. To deliberately bait me like that."

"So you decided to take the bait," my mother said.

"Mom, I didn't decide anything. It's like I just couldn't help myself, I was beyond mad. And look, the dirty martinis and champagne probably didn't help matters, I'll admit that."

"So you were mad at her, not Gordon?" I asked, hoping poor Gordon could escape time in the doghouse.

"I was furious that the bitch had so little respect for me that she would flaunt herself in front of me like that. I guess it pissed me off she had discounted me, because I'm not twenty two. Because I'm only a middle-aged mom. I think my pride was hurt more than anything else. But I was also mad at Gordon. I still am. I know on one level it's not his fault that young girls throw themselves at him. I understand that. For God's sake, look at him. He's like catnip to those young girls."

"But still," I said.

"Yes, but still, he could do a little more to fend them off. Out of respect to me and our marriage." Deirdre took a sip of her coffee. "I know he loves me, and I can't imagine he would ever go beyond flirting. But it's been happening for years. When I was young and pretty, it didn't bother me. I was probably as much of a flirt as he was. But now that I'm older, it's different."

"So what are you going to do?" my mother asked, somewhat bewildered. I didn't think it would occur to my gentle giant of a father to flirt with a woman, so my mother had never faced such a situation. Of course with his trademark Griffin ginger hair and large nose, it's not like the ladies were breaking down his door. Grace, who shared Deirdre's blond curls and petite frame, was the gorgeous one in that relationship.

"I think I'm going to let him sweat it out a bit. Teach him a lesson," Deirdre said with spirit. The Advil must've kicked in.

"How?" I asked.

"I'm going to make him stay with his mother. A few days sleeping in her basement and eating her dry pork chops and he'll come running home with his tail behind him."

"Don't push him too far, Dee. Look what happened to me," I said.

"I'm not worried about Gordon. He's not going anywhere. Plus, I don't think he could find Australia on a map if his life depended on it." She laughed.

"Kate's right, Deirdre. You don't want to push him into anyone else's arms," my mother said. "Be careful."

"Okay, maybe I won't make him sleep at his mother's. Maybe I'll just go on a big shopping spree instead."

"Don't do that either," my mother said. "You'll come crying to me when the bill comes. Why do you have to play these games? Why don't you tell him you're fed up with his flirting, that he's gone too far this time?"

"Yeah, Dee. Honesty, what a concept."

"You might want to try a bit of it yourself, miss," my mother said, turning to me. "Does this Paul character even know you're married? Is he married?"

"Mom, I've spoken with him a total of four times. We danced. That's it. We haven't exchanged our bios."

"He's definitely interested in you. You should have seen how he looked at her, Mom. His eyes never left her, even when she was across the room dancing with us."

"He doesn't even have my number or know where I live. Now that the show is over, I probably won't see him again."

"Oh yeah. I can't imagine how he'd find you. Ever hear of the internet?"

"You know what," I said, "I'm having another coffee and more of these delicious eggs, and then I'm spending the rest of the day on the couch, resting my battered back. I'm not thinking about errant husbands, potential boyfriends, the horrible Wives or cats. Dee, I suggest you go home and do the same."

"You're right, Kate, pour me out some coffee before I go."

"Fill me up too," my mother said, holding out her cup.

Chapter 10

It took me almost a week to decompress after the finale. Tom and crew came by the following week and dismantled all of the "hidden" cameras and microphones. I told Tom he was going to miss me and, to my surprise, he agreed. As he left my kitchen for the last time, he jokingly said he'd see me during season two. I gave him a hug and rumpled his messy hair. Over my dead body.

I finally wrote Jim a serious email about the end of our marriage. I told him that since he had been gone six months, I was filing a petition for divorce on the grounds of abandonment. I didn't receive a reply email, but he did call once when I was at the movies with Angela and my parents were babysitting. He spoke with Lucy. Unfortunately, the call only further confused the poor child. For some reason Lucy had gotten it into her head that Jim was dead and in heaven. She insisted for days afterward that Daddy had called her from heaven.

As Deirdre had predicted, Paul Goodman tracked down my address and phone number. He called me several times, but, chicken that I am, I never answered. I may not look like Grace, but in many ways I am my mother's daughter and share her ingrained Catholic mores. It was bad enough I was getting divorced. It simply wasn't in me to start a relationship before I was legally separated. Paul stopped calling, but he did send a stunning arrangement of yellow roses. The card said he'd enjoyed our short time together and hoped to hear from me when I was ready. I sent him a thank you note, putting that little romantic chapter of my life to rest.

Two days later, as I was Windexing my living room's bay windows, I saw an unfamiliar SUV pull into my driveway. Curious, I put down my paper towels and watched as a blonde with long hair awkwardly climbed out of the SUV, straightened her tight skirt and marched up my stone walkway. The Windex fumes must have gotten to me--this had to be my imagination. It couldn't be.

"Hello, Elaine," I said, opening the door before she could knock. "This is a surprise."

"Hello, Kate. You're looking well," she said, clearly ignoring the bandana in my hair. "Can I come in?"

"Of course." I stepped aside and allowed her to enter. This should be good. "Coffee?"

"That would be nice," Elaine said as she followed me into the kitchen.

I took my time getting the coffee together. I cut us both a slice of cheesecake. Elaine said nothing, although she smiled at me when I poured her a cup of coffee.

"So." I sat across from Elaine.

"I hope you don't mind me just dropping by. I thought I should tell you this in person."

"Tell me what?"

"I have some good news. Our sales department found a new sponsor for the show." Who, Poligrip? Bail bondsmen? "They've seen the show's rough footage and are very excited about the show."

"Great," I said without inflection.

"It *is* great. They're interested in a product placement arrangement."

"How can you do that now that filming is over?"

"That's why I'm here. We want to shoot a bonus episode. This week if possible."

"I'm sure the other girls will love to shoot another episode." I poured her some more coffee.

"Yes, they are excited."

"Terrific. Good luck with that."

"The new sponsors want all four Wives to participate."

I gave her a big, insincere smile. "Well, I guess you'd better go on out there and find another fool to cast because this fool is done."

"Kate, I know the finale did not go, uh, smoothly."

"There's an understatement if I've ever heard one. Another slice of cake?"

"Kate, what can I do to make you say yes? It will be one night, two days tops."

"There is really nothing you can say," I said. "More coffee?"

Elaine's eyes narrowed. "Five thousand. I can offer you five thousand."

"Sorry. Not enough."

"Seven."

"No thanks."

"Fifteen. I can offer you fifteen and no more. Take it or leave it."

Fifteen thousand would buy me five more months of mortgage payments. After a few moments, I said, "Fifteen, after tax. You take it or leave it."

"Fine," Elaine said. I wondered whether she had been willing to go up to twenty. Oh well, too late now.

I sighed. "Okay, what do I have to do?"

"Not much. Our two new sponsors are Long Island Ferry and Wolf Lodge Casino. All you need to do is take the ferry across to Connecticut and then spend the night in a suite at Wolf Lodge. The casino will give you another two thousand dollars in chips, but you need to gamble with them, not cash them in."

"I want my own hotel room."

"It will be a very large suite, plenty of room for the four of you. We need to see some interaction."

"Based on prior experience, I'm sure *interaction* will not be a problem. I'm not staying in the same room with those three. And since I can almost guarantee they'll either yell at me or ignore me, I want Angela and Dee to come with me. I want a separate suite for the three of us."

"Kate, I've talked to the other Wives, and they've promised they'll be nice."

"Yeah, right. Angela and Dee come with me, or I'm not going."

"Fine."

"And they get gambling chips and Chris picks out new outfits for us."

"Anything else?"

"And we get our own limo."

"No, Kate, you have to interact with the other Wives at some point. I'll send your sister and Angela in their own limo. But you will ride with the other three, and then all six of you will take the ferry together."

I thought about it for a moment. Oh, what the hell. It was only an hour ride to the ferry. I could deal with anything for an hour. "Okay, fine."

Elaine looked relieved. She fished a two page document out of her bag and laid it on my kitchen table. "I just need you to sign this addendum to your contract."

"Send it to my lawyer."

"Kate, I really..."

"No buts, Elaine. Send it to Glenn Meyers. There is no trust here, and I'm not signing a thing without his okay." Elaine may not be the brightest bulb, but even she knew when she was about to push someone too far.

"Okay, Kate, okay. I'll send it over to him this afternoon, and I'll tell Chris to get some outfits together." She handed me a sheet of paper. "Here's the shooting schedule. We'll pick you up Thursday morning."

"Fantastic. Can't wait."

"Oh, Kate, I knew I could bring you around." She gave me a wide, almost sincere smile. "You'll have a great time, I know you will." She really was an idiot.

Angela heard about the Wolf Lodge trip and had been angling for an invite, so she was in. Deirdre still wasn't talking to Gordon, so the thought of time spent drinking and gambling while he was stuck carting the children to their numerous activities sounded good to her. When I told my parents about the extra fifteen grand Channel 45 was offering, they were happy to babysit Lucy. We were all set.

God help us.

* * * *

At ten to eleven on Thursday morning, the limo pulled up the driveway. Rachel was already in the back of the limo. Tom, armed with a small hand-held camera, sat in the front. I clambered past Rachel and sat in the back of the limo facing forward so that my motion sickness wouldn't be triggered. "Good morning, Rachel."

Silence. Well, so much for the girls being nice.

Next we picked up Tina who, clad in a gold tank top and black skinny jeans, looked like she was ready to party. She seemed unsure as to who to sit next to. She sat across from me on the small jump seat behind the driver, her Switzerland status thus maintained.

"Hi, girls," Tina said in her breathy, baby girl voice. "Are you ready to win some money?"

"Absolutely," I said, with a big, fake smile.

"How about you, Rachel?" Tina asked.

"I'm still recovering from the LICKs Ball," she said in full martyr mode, "and what with our new furniture line coming out, I've been absolutely swamped. This wasn't the best time for me. But, Elaine begged me, so what could I do?"

"You're a real team player, Rachel," I said without inflection.

Rachel graced me with her most fearsome bitchface and then ignored me the rest of the trip.

Fifteen minutes later we pulled up to Pamela's estate. Tom hopped out of the front seat of the limo and rang her doorbell. Twenty minutes later they emerged, poor Tom weighed down by two suitcases. Pamela carried her makeup bag.

Pamela sat next to me and decided to be friendly. She asked about my husband and my sister. After exchanging a dozen meaningless pleasantries, she turned to speak to Rachel. I zoned out and watched the exits fly by.

Fifty minutes later we pulled into Long Island Ferry's pitted gravel parking lot. The stench of diesel fuel assaulted me as I climbed out of the limo, my stomach churning from the trip and the tension. Angela, outfitted in a leather miniskirt and leopard pumps, was perched on a wooden bench, her foot tapping to the Timbaland blaring from her iPod.

"Hey, girls!" Angela shouted over her music. "Love the necklace, Pam!" It was then I noticed Pamela was sporting a kissing owl pendant. Interesting.

"Hi, Angela. Love your shoes!" Pamela said with equal enthusiasm. It looked like we had a mutual admiration society going on here. "I'm glad you could make it. Why didn't you ride with us?"

"I came with Deirdre," Angela replied.

Pamela, trying to suppress a grimace, said, "Oh."

"Where is Dee anyway?" I asked.

"In there, getting coffee." Angela pointed to the battered snack shack.

"I'd better help her," I said, escaping the owls and the Wives.

Deirdre, tapping her foot in irritation, stood at the end of a long line of caffeine-deprived retirees. "If I have to hear one more thing about Angela's owls, I swear I'll jump off that damn boat."

"Please, your trip couldn't possibly have been as bad as mine. I don't know what made me sicker, the motion sickness or Pamela's attempts at polite conversation."

"You're not still getting car sick, are you?" Deirdre said in exasperation. "What are you, five?"

"Let's just hope I don't get boat sick on top of it. That's all I need, an episode devoted to my barfing."

"Hives, barfing--the health department's gonna put you in quarantine."

"Girls, are you ordering or chatting?" snarled the seventy-year-old snack bar lady.

"Three large coffees, light and sweet," Deirdre said.

"And three powdered donuts," I added.

We walked back to the bench where Angela was holding court before the Wives and the cameras. Pamela was laughing when she noticed us. "Oh, thank God. Coffee."

"Sorry, Pamela. This is Angela's coffee," Deirdre said, handing Angela the styrofoam cup."

"Oh, sweetie, you can have mine." Angela handed Pamela her cup. Deirdre didn't even attempt to hide her scowl. The battered ferry blew its horn.

"Ladies," Tom said, "could you please board the ferry now?"

Deirdre and I trailed the other four, who linked their arms as if climbing aboard the Queen Mary. Once onboard, the smell of fuel mixed with grease from the ferry's snack bar. The stench, together with the stale donut and weak coffee, did a number on my stomach. I grabbed a seat on the outside deck and took deep breaths of the briny sea air. The other girls, not wanting to mess up their hair, stayed inside with the fumes.

Twenty minutes into the trip, Elaine joined me outside. I hadn't even been aware she was on the boat. "This isn't exactly what I meant by interaction, Kate."

"Unless you want my lunch to interact with your shoes, I suggest you leave me alone," I said, without taking my eye off of the distant horizon.

"I hope you feel better soon. We only have one night here, and I want our sponsors to get their money's worth."

"I can't imagine that vomit is going to do much for ticket sales. Why don't you and the cameras head back inside."

As much as I think Elaine would have loved to shoot another embarrassing scene of me, she left. Thirty minutes later, the ferry lurched into its docking space, and the six of us climbed down narrow metal steps into the depressing port of New London, Connecticut. Two limos were waiting, and Dee, Angela and I took the first limo along with Tom.

"Oh, so you're joining us," Deirdre said to Angela.

"Of course I am," Angela said, her eyes wide and innocent.

"I thought maybe you'd want to ride with your new best friend."

"Please, Dee, I was only trying to be friendly. We have to hang with them tonight, so we might as well make the best of it. Besides, anyone who likes my owls can't be all bad."

"Are you kidding me, Ang? Have you forgotten the finale?"

"Deirdre," Angela said, shaking her head, "she's not the one who kissed your husband. I think you're being unfair."

Deirdre's fair cheeks burned with temper, but before she could speak I said, "You're right, Angela. It can't hurt to be pleasant. Let's just try and make this as painless as possible."

"Angela, I think you should remember it was Kate who invited you, not Pamela."

"Oh, Katie knows how much I love her," Angela said, giving me a hug that only worsened my motion sickness.

Two hours later the six of us, decked out in the slinky cocktail dresses Chris had selected, stood next to an enormous teepee. The sweatpants-clad seniors barely noticed us as they shuffled to the all-you-can eat buffet located behind the teepee. We tried to appear casual and natural as we chatted--or at least appeared to chat--next to a *Welcome to Wolf Lodge Casino* sign. After the photo op, Elaine rewarded us with two thousand dollars' worth of complimentary chips and told us our time was our own as long as we stayed within the main casino area and met at the Peroquot Paragon restaurant at eight o'clock for dinner.

Dee and I headed to the blackjack table while the others hit the craps table, but not before Angela trilled, "Sweetie, I'm hopeless at cards. You don't mind if I try the dice, do ya?" and was gone before I could respond.

"How pissed are you?" Deirdre asked.

"I really don't care, to tell you the truth. Let the four musketeers have their fun, so long as the Griffin girls make some money. Oh, Dee, you got an ace!"

"Monkey, monkey," said the man sitting next to us.

I remembered from my last Caribbean cruise with Jim that *monkey* was some type of Asian term for twenty-one, or maybe it meant an ace--whatever, I thought it meant something good. "Yeah, give us two monkeys," I said as I pulled an ace too.

Two hours later we were all up, me by about two hundred dollars, Deirdre by five hundred and Mr. Monkey by at least eight hundred. I could hear Rachel's braying laughter across the casino, so I assumed at least one of them was doing well. The last time I had walked past them on the way to the bathroom, Angela and Pamela had been drinking champagne with two guys in suits. Tina had been chatting with some college guys.

Pamela startled me by asking, "This seat free?"

"Um, sure."

"I'm not having much luck at craps. How do you play this again?"

"You need to reach twenty-one, hence the name," Deirdre said without looking up from her cards.

"Oh, of course," Pamela said as she took out her chips. Tom and a camera man quietly moved behind us.

We played a few rounds. Pamela took hits when she shouldn't have, causing Mr. Monkey to stomp off in disgust. Pamela got a pair of eights and was about to take a hit when Deirdre snapped, "For God's sake Pamela, split those."

"What do you mean?"

"It's a losing hand," I said. "People usually split eights."

"Oh, okay," she said. She pulled a ten and a nine, not great, but better than what she had. The dealer made twenty, so everyone except Deirdre lost.

"How're you doing, sweetie?" Rachel said, as she took Mr. Monkey's chair.

"Don't take advice from those two. They cost me two hundred dollars." No good deed goes unpunished.

"Why would I take their advice about anything?" Rachel said, as she placed a fifty dollar bet.

"Hello? I'm not deaf," Deirdre said to her back. "I'm sitting right here."

Rachel ignored her and pulled a six.

I picked up my chips. "Come on, Dee, let's go."

"No way! You and I were here first, and we were winning. Let that cow leave."

"Really, Deirdre, is it necessary to talk like that?" Pamela admonished. "Let's have a friendly little game."

"Hey, did the party move over here?" Angela asked, dragging Tina and an underage admirer with her.

"Here, girls, take our seats," I said.

Angela slid her lycra-encased bottom onto my seat. "Okay, if you're sure."

"I'm sure."

After Deirdre and I threw a few hundred in the slots without much luck, we went back to the suite to freshen up for dinner. I had just sprayed my hair when Deirdre asked, "Exactly how much crap do you plan on taking from those bitches tonight?"

"Dee, it's a big place. Let's keep moving. If the other girls play blackjack, we'll play the slots."

"But we were winning at that table."

"So what? It's the casino's money anyway. It's like monopoly money."

"Well, I wouldn't mind taking some of that monopoly money home. But what about dinner? We can't just get up in the middle of dinner and leave if they start up with us."

"Let's stay relaxed," I said. "I know it's hard. Don't let them bait you."

"It would be nice if we weren't outnumbered. What the hell is up with Angela?"

"I think she wants to keep the peace." I sprayed on some perfume.

"Bullshit," Dee snapped. "She just wants to be the next Gold Coast Wife. Can't you see that's why she's sucking up to Pamela?"

"She and Pamela were always friendly."

"Yeah, maybe in high school. Honestly, how many times has Angela seen her since graduation? She wasn't even at Angela's wedding, and I think Angela invited every person she ever said hello to. How good of friends could they have been?"

"I don't know," I said with a sigh. "Does it matter?"

"Yes, it matters. You invited Angela to give you support, not to kiss Pamela Reynolds's ass. Kate, how long are you going to let her shit all over you?"

"Look, I hear what you're saying. I do. But let's not blow it out of proportion."

"It's just like the lunchroom at Queen of the Rosary," she spat out in disgust. "You were grateful for any crumb Angela threw your way."

"What are you talking about?"

"How many times did she ever sit with you and eat lunch? Be honest, how many?"

I sat on the bed. "We ate lunch together," I said in a small voice.

"No you didn't. Sure, she'd stop by, and maybe sit a few minutes. Long enough to say hello and get a copy of your homework. But she always went back to the cheerleaders' table."

"Not always," I said, trying not to sound too pathetic.

"Yes, always."

"What would you like me to do now, Deirdre? Drag her away from the craps table and make her sit with us?"

"I would love to see you stand up for yourself. For once."

"Please, I'm a hedge fund lawyer, not exactly a shrinking violet."

"Sure, you stand up for your clients. What about for yourself? Have you ever stood up to Mom, Angela, Jim?"

"I don't want to talk about Jim. Not tonight."

"Fine, we won't talk about Jim. What about Angela?"

"What about me?" Angela asked, walking through the door.

"Oh," I said looking up. "I wanted to know if we should wait for you, but here you are."

"Sorry I'm late, sweetie. I was on a hot streak. I won almost five hundred bucks. Pammy won even more than that!"

"Awesome," Deirdre said with venom.

"What's up your ass, Dee?" Angela said as she walked to the mirror and took out her lipstick.

"Nothing," I said before she could answer, "nothing. We're just hungry."

"Oh," Angela said, turning to give us a big smile, "I know how you Griffin girls get about food. I'll be only a minute."

"Don't," I said to Deirdre under my breath, "just don't. Let it go."

* * * *

The Wolf Lodge's *Indian Maidens* performed an interpretive dance where I think they were supposed to be chasing a deer or something, while the six of us and the assorted *Gold Coast Wives* crew watched and ate overcooked shrimp. I wasn't aware that traditional Native American garb included spandex and push-up bras, but hey, whatever, A for effort and all. A shirtless "warrior" beat haphazardly on a drum and made eyes at Tina.

"Oh, that was wonderful, just wonderful," Pamela said when Elaine gave her the signal.

"Yes," chimed in Rachel, "very informative."

"Very rhythmic," Tina purred to her new admirer.

The entertainment left as the waiters brought our salads. Rachel droned on about her new furniture collection, and then Angela took over and regaled us with her latest "design" ideas. Boring but not controversial and not directed at me. So, fairly happy and content, I chewed my charred t-bone.

"Pamela," Dee said during a lull in the conversation, "you'll never believe who I ran into last week."

"Who?" Pamela didn't look up from her vegetarian lasagna.

"Carol Ann Leonard. You know, from Queen of the Rosary? We used to play tennis together."

"Carol Ann? Why, I haven't thought of her in years."

"That's surprising. Weren't you two roommates? She told me you shared a one bedroom in the East 80s before you got married."

Pamela's mouth tightened ever so slightly. "Oh, well, you know how busy you get with a new husband and baby. It's hard to stay in touch."

"She said to give you her regards. In fact, she's still living in the same apartment. We had lunch there last Monday. Unusual decor--I felt like I was in a dungeon. Anyway, Carol Ann told me some really interesting stories about you. She also showed me some photos."

Where the hell was Deirdre going with this? "Drop it," I whispered.

Pamela kept her remote, superior smile in place, although she turned a few shades paler under her meticulous makeup.

Reaching inside her purse, Deirdre smiled. "I didn't realize you were such a party girl, Pam." She flung a half-dozen photos across the table.

Oh, my.

There was silence until Rachel said, "What a funny Halloween costume, Pamela."

Deirdre sprinkled a few more photos across the table. "Halloween? You must like Halloween a lot, Pam. It's funny how you always pick the same type of costume. What, did you buy leather pasties in bulk?"

"I, uh, well..."

"Oh, look, here's a cute one of you and Carol Ann."

How should I describe this? Carol Ann was wearing a studded leather dog collar, a leather bustier and ripped fishnet stockings. Pamela was topless and, except for the leather pasties, a thong, and high black leather boots, wasn't wearing much else. Carol Ann was grabbing Pamela's breast as Pamela was laughing.

In the other photos, Pamela was wearing black leather, and there were one or more scantily-clothed women with her. Someone was usually holding a whip of some sort.

Tina said quietly, "Pamela, it's okay. Everyone experiments when they're young."

"Of course," Rachel said. "Why, I remember my first summer at sleep-away camp, one of the counselors..."

"Yeah," Deirdre interrupted, "except Pamela wasn't exactly young when she took these pictures. She was in her thirties at least." My sister handed Tina and Rachel a few more photos. "And it wasn't only with women. Carol Ann told me that a few years after she first opened her--what did she call it? Oh, yeah, her *private club*,--she allowed men to join. Apparently Mistress Beverley was quite popular with both the ladies and the men. Lots of men. Some rather successful and important men."

Another dozen photos lay on Deirdre's lap, one with a familiar bald man dressed in a garter. She was about to hand this one to Tina, but I stopped her.

"Enough, Dee. That's enough."

"Enough? I'm only getting started. There are lots more pictures, Pamela, but you know that, don't you?"

Pamela was beyond speechless--I think she was approaching catatonic. I yanked Deirdre off her chair and dragged her out of the private dining room.

"Are you out of your mind?" I hissed as I pulled her past the other diners.

"You hit me, I'm gonna hit you back. Only harder. She should have known better than to mess with me. But you ruined it, Kate. You completely ruined it. I was about to show them the pictures of Don. Carol

Ann says he was their best customer. Actually he was Carol Ann's best customer before Pamela stole him away from her."

"Thank God I stopped you."

"Why, Kate?" Deirdre asked as we left the restaurant and entered the casino. "Why did you stop me?"

"Do you know what this would do to Don if it got out? What it would do to his company?"

"Serves him right for marrying such an evil bitch."

"Then what about me? Don is one of the most powerful members of the hedge fund industry. What do you think would happen if you made those pictures public? I'd never work in hedge funds again!"

"Oh, I didn't think of that."

"No, clearly you didn't."

We walked in silence to the Peroquot Bar and ordered two martinis. After we finished, I ordered another round.

"Kate," Deirdre said midway through her second martini, "I'm sorry. I really am. I wanted to get back at her for how she treated us at the finale. I thought you'd be happy."

"You went too far."

"I know. I know. I'm a hothead."

"I invited you and Angela because I thought you'd make things easier, shield me from them. Instead, Angela kissed their asses and you, well you threw a nuclear bomb at Pamela. I should have come here on my own." I gulped the remainder of my martini.

"Kate, I know. I'm sorry." A few moments later she added, "But can you believe Rachel wanted to talk about her teenage lesbian experiences?" She laughed. "Come on, you have to admit that was funny."

"God, she's such a sheep. I swear, if you had told her Pamela was into necrophilia, she would have brought up that time at her grandmother's funeral when she felt all tingly."

"Oh my God, that's gross."

"What's gross?" Angela asked as she slid onto the bar stool next to Dee.

"You don't want to know."

"Where are your buddies, Ang?" Deirdre asked.

"Dee, I can't believe those pictures! Why didn't you say something earlier?"

"I wanted it to be a surprise. So where are your buds?"

"Rachel had to go home early, some type of furniture emergency. I don't know. And Pamela, she wasn't feeling too good and went back to the suite."

"Since the cool girls are gone, you thought you'd hang with the Griffin girls? Seems like old times," Deirdre said.

"Oh, don't be like that." Angela swatted her arm. "I was only trying to be nice. I can't believe it though. What a whore! My Jerry's gonna kill me when he finds out I let a prostitute in our house, around our children."

"Come on," I said, "in fairness, we don't know she took money, only that she was a bit, well, a bit wild."

Angela held up her foot. "Kate, wearing leopard print pumps is a bit wild. Whipping businessmen with your top off, that's prostitution."

I gulped the remainder of my martini. "I'll bet you anything either Channel 45 never airs this, or if they do, Pamela will come out smelling like a rose while me and Deirdre will be the bad guys. Believe me, there are some people in this world you just can't beat, and I've finally accepted that Pamela Reynolds is one of them."

"I don't know, Kate, those pictures were pretty explicit," Deirdre said.

"If they do show them, six months from now she'll be selling Mistress Beverley lingerie and fur-lined handcuffs on QVC. Mark my words. Do we want one more?"

"Oh, Tom wants us to join Tina in the Teepee dance club," Angela said. "I hope he's not mad--I told him I'd bring you right over."

"Dancing?" I waved to the bartender. "I definitely need another drink."

Chapter 11

Lucy and I returned from our Monday morning dance class where one of the yummy mummies asked if I wanted to join their Starbucks coffee pool. Of course I said yes and handed her my twenty. After being excluded by the Wives for the past few weeks, it was a relief to feel some type of acceptance and belonging, even if only a coffee klatch in the YMCA's drafty hallway. I was taking off Lucy's denim jacket when the doorbell rang.

"What are you doing here?" I asked Deirdre, who was standing on the steps holding a box of pastries from Giamelli's.

She handed me the pastry box. "Well, hello to you too. State testing. The senior teachers have the day off. If I stayed home I'd feel guilty about not catching up on the laundry, so I figured I'd drop by."

"Come in, come in." I closed the door behind her. "Coffee or tea?"

"Tea. I'm coffee'd out."

"Yeah, me too," and I told her about my recent induction into the yummy mummy coffee club.

Deirdre laughed. "I can't believe you're excited. I belong to about four coffee clubs. You are so weird. I don't understand how you ever got along with all those lawyers and bankers when a few moms in stretchy pants leave you a quivering mess."

"I know. I'm pathetic. Look, I worked with mostly men--there wasn't as much subcontext. I never worried whether they liked me or not, and I usually knew where I stood with them, at least I did before the Barry debacle last fall. With all the air kissing and talking about whose son can read and whose daughter can do long division at age three, it's too much. I never know what to say."

"You'd never last at Hadley Middle School, that's for sure." Deirdre bit into a cheese danish.

"I know." I laughed as I poured out the tea. "Have you let Gordon out of jail yet?"

"Dr. Phil would be very proud of me. After the limo dropped me off on Friday, we engaged in *open and honest communication*. I told him how the constant flirting bothered me, and I how I felt uncomfortable with him coaching the girls varsity soccer team."

"I didn't know the coaching bothered you."

"Oh, please. Teenage girls always running around in their little shorts. Plus, they call the house constantly, manufacturing reasons to talk to him," she said with disgust. "Oh, Coach Pederson," she said in high breathy voice, "which shin guards should I bring to practice? Oh, Coach Pederson, can I book a private practice session with you?"

"I can see how that could be annoying. What did he say?"

"He cried. Can you believe it? Cool Mr. Jock actually cried. Gordon said he had no idea his flirting upset me. He apologized for being such an idiot, and he called the principal and requested he coach the boys junior varsity team next year."

"Wow."

"Yeah, I think I really scared him at the LICKs Ball. And then taking off for the casino with you pushed him over the edge. He begged me not to kick him out."

"So you forgave him?"

"Yes, of course I forgave him. But I'm not stupid. I told him we're selling those ridiculous jet skis collecting dust in the garage, I'm renovating the kitchen in the fall and he'd better not make any more big purchases without my okay. I also negotiated an extra night out a week and signed up for a pilates class."

"And he agreed?"

"Of course he agreed. He even thanked me. I suppose fear of living in a basement will do that to you."

"You are officially my hero."

"Sometimes you have to treat men like the dogs that they are," she said with a smirk.

"I'm not sure Dr. Phil would agree with you, but hey, whatever works." The doorbell rang. "Geez, it's like Grand Central Station in here today."

"Have you read it?" Angela gushed when I opened the door.

"Read what?"

"The review? The review of *Gold Coast Wives* in *Long Island News*. It's on the front page of the Arts section."

"Only in *Long Island News* would a reality show constitute art."

"Oh, please, Kate, you are such a snob."

"And proud of it. I think I was twelve the last time I read the *Long Island News*."

"Oh whatever, Miss Georgetown. So it's not *The Times*," Angela said. "Hey, Dee! Why aren't you in school?"

"State testing. Danish?"

"Oh, no, I'm officially on a diet now that I saw the *Gold Coast Wives* raw footage."

"If you look fat, then I'd better wire my mouth shut." I took another bite of danish.

"Did I look fat?" a worried Deirdre asked.

"Looking fat is the least of your worries, Miss Muhammad Ali," Angela said.

"Oh, please, I didn't hit that slut. I only shoved her a little."

"The tape don't lie, my friend."

"How bad did I look?" I asked as I poured Angela a cup of tea.

"I only saw the finale. I have to say, though, I thought you looked pretty good. Of course Chris took all the credit for your transformation. He told Elaine he thought you looked luscious. Even Jerry thought you looked good--he called you juicy."

"Juicy and luscious. What am I, a plum?"

"I thought you looked good too," my sister conceded. "The dress did wonders for you." I think that was meant as a compliment.

"You're lucky Channel 45 used your picture from the finale in the *Long Island News* article," Angela said as she opened the paper to the Arts section.

"Oh, my God. The review covers the whole page!" I grabbed the paper.

"Kate," Deirdre said with awe, "you look amazing."

"Who cares what I look like? There wasn't supposed to be all this publicity. Chris told me the show would only be viewed by prison inmates!"

"Apparently the execs at Channel 45 were surprised by how well the show tested within the key demographics and what with the product placement deals they struck with Wolf Lodge and the Long Island Ferry, the station had money to promote it. Elaine is riding high from the buzz, and Chris thinks he might be able to host his own makeover show after this," Angela said.

"'*Gold Coast Wives* is a warts-and-all behind the scenes look at the privileged lives of Long Island's elite,'" Deirdre read. "Oh, here's where they mention you, Kate."

Kate Ryan, a plus-sized former lawyer with a serious donut obsession, clashes with her more glamorous cast mates, especially her high school nemesis, Pamela Kruger, wife of multi-millionaire hedge fund manager Don Kruger.

Also known as Mistress Beverly." Deirdre giggled. "No, I'm kidding. It doesn't really say that."

"Just keep reading," I said.

"Okay."

Devastated by the disappearance of her husband and crippled by her many insecurities, Kate lashes out at the more beautiful and successful Wives.

"Oh man," she said, "that's not good."

"Plus-sized? Are they kidding me? Since when is size fourteen considered plus size?" I cried.

"Actually, size sixteen," Angela said. "Chris told me the red dress you wore to the finale was a size sixteen."

"Whatever. Sure I've gained a few pounds, but I'm hardly a blimp."

"Of course you're not," Angela said.

"You're just healthy," Deirdre added. *Healthy* was our mother's codeword for fat.

"Shut up, Dee," I snapped. "You're not helping."

"Sorry," she said, not sounding a bit sorry.

I pushed away the plate of half-eaten danish. "Did the article mention either of you?"

"Oh," Angela said, "not really."

"I assume by 'not really' you mean yes. It's okay, you can tell me. I've already been called insecure and plus-sized. I can take it."

"The article called me a 'petite powerhouse' and an 'up and coming jewelry designer,'" Angela said.

"Fantastic. And you?" I glared at Deirdre. "What did the article say about you?"

"'Warm and goodhearted.'"

"I'm sure they said something about your looks too," I pressed. "What did it say?"

"They said I had an 'understated sex appeal' and called me 'angelic.'"

"Angelic? Sure, when you're not beating up adolescents or outing a secret dominatrix. Well, that's great. I'm happy for you. Really. You guys have to leave now so I can turn on the gas."

"Come on, Kate," Angela said, "it's not that bad. It's still only a local newspaper. None of your fancy lawyer friends will see it."

"Let's hope not. So when does this train wreck air?"

"The editors have been working nonstop on the editing. The first episode will air on Thursday. Chris is throwing a viewing party at his place. Do you want to come?"

"God, no. I don't think I'm even going to watch it."

"She'll watch it," Deirdre said to Angela. "How could she not?"

"If I do watch it, I'm not watching it in front of an audience. I'm going to cry in peace."

With a box of donuts.

Chapter 12

Well, I didn't come off looking too good in the first episode, and the second and third episodes of *Gold Coast Wives* weren't much better. The cameras seemed to have caught every one of Lucy's meltdowns, every instance of me bribing her with cookies, every sharp word I said to my mother and every awkward moment between myself and the other Wives. The cameras even caught a conversation with Deirdre where I had mocked my annoying mother-in-law. I was fairly certain no humanitarian of the year awards would be headed my way anytime soon.

Initially, I consoled myself with the fact that no one would probably watch this ridiculous show. That illusion was soon shattered after I made my weekly trip to the dry cleaners. Normally, the cranky dry cleaner lady and her sulky underachieving teenage daughter would avoid eye contact whenever I dropped off our clothes. The old bat was usually too busy complaining about her bastard ex-husband and late alimony payments. Which is fine. As far as I could tell, she never talked to any of her other customers either, so I was spared the trouble of making idle chitchat. However, this time when I entered, the teenage daughter giggled at me and ran in the back to get her mother.

With a flourish I had never seen before, the cranky mommy dry cleaner handed me my dry cleaning before I'd even produced my ticket. "Mrs. Ryan, here you go. I hope everything is to your liking. Now, will you need extra starch in these collars?"

"Um, er, no. I don't think so."

"Kate? Can I call you Kate? Kate, I wanted to tell you I absolutely love your new show. I can't believe we have such a famous customer," she simpered and made a grimace that I assume was meant to be a pleasant smile.

"Of course, you can call me Kate. And really, it's not a big deal, it's only a local cable show."

"My friends are addicted to it," gushed the daughter, "and my boyfriend's dorm mates at Hofstra came up with a drinking game to play while watching it."

"Oh, what's the game?" I asked, dreading the answer.

"Every time you eat a donut or a piece of cake or call someone a bitch, the boys do a shot."

"How charming."

"And every time Tina flashes some boob, they drink a funnel of beer."

"Sounds like fun," I said with a groan.

"Oh, it is. The party is getting so big that next week they're moving it over to the local fraternity house!"

"Fantastic. Can I have my change now?"

"Tell me, Kate," the mommy dry cleaner asked, "is Gordon as delicious in person as he is on TV?"

"Even more so."

"Tell him if he ever needs any dry cleaning done, we'll give him our friends and family discount." Her eye spasmed in what I think was supposed to be a playful wink.

"I'm sure my sister will appreciate that."

"Kate," said the daughter, "can I have your autograph?"

After signing autographs for sulky girl and the brothers of Sigma Sigma Epsilon, I grabbed my dry cleaning and made a hasty escape.

The next Monday at Lucy's dance class, my new coffee buddies were all a-twitter.

"Kate, I can't believe you were holding out on us all this time," scolded Melissa Green, Marion's former Bunco friend.

"I take it you all saw the show?" I asked, looking around at their excited, over-caffeinated faces.

"Of course we saw it!" said Ellie Walters, a perky blonde in her early thirties. "It's so exciting! You have to tell us what it was like."

"Exhausting and annoying more than anything else. Really, guys, it was no big deal. My friend's brother works on the show, and the producers were looking for an 'every woman' to offset the fabulosity of the other Wives. For some reason they picked me."

"I can't believe you were on a show with Camilla Yardley. Did she tell you when she was getting out of the coma?"

"Is Pamela as beautiful in person as she is on TV?"

And the questions pretty much continued in that vein for the rest of the dance class. The dance yummies couldn't seem to hear enough about the show. I guess any contact with TV, even a sad little cable TV show, is exciting to some people. To be honest, if I were in their shoes I'd probably find it exciting too, and my questions would probably be even more stupid. I was surprised none of them mentioned how I was portrayed, but I was certain it had been the topic of many a Bunco game.

Wherever I went during those first three weeks, it seemed I was met either with puzzled looks, as if the person thought they knew me from somewhere but couldn't quite place me, or people recognized me, the shy ones simply smiling and the bold ones asking me questions. One blond bimbalina even asked if Gordon and my sister had broken up yet.

With a mixture of trepidation that I might be recognized as a Gold Coast Wife and hope that I would be remembered as a respected member of the hedge fund bar, I walked into the main ballroom of the Waldorf Astoria to the tenth annual New York Asset Managers Symposium.

I always thought it strange that people think of the Waldorf as such a swanky hotel. I'd attended so many conferences and seminars there that it held no more appeal for me than a Fowler Sherman conference room. I met Shari at the welcome table. I couldn't help but be mortified by my name badge, the badge that simply said *Kate Ryan* this year and pretty much announced I was unemployed. Since Shari had a half hour free before her presentation on anti-money laundering regulations, she joined me for coffee and a mini-bagel. We kept the conversation light and discussed our children and summer plans. I got the sense she was embarrassed she had not been able to help me more on the job search front. I was relieved that she evidently hadn't yet heard of my escapades as a Gold Coast Wife. Maybe Chris was right--*Gold Coast Wives* was just a stupid cable show no one outside of Long Island would ever know about.

After promising to meet up at the cocktail party later that afternoon, Shari rushed off to her seminar. I wandered over to mine on Hedge Fund Adviser Regulation, which wasn't scheduled to start for another half hour. I chatted amiably with a few of the other attendees, many of whom I'd met at various functions over the years. I didn't get any strange looks or odd questions about Camilla Yardley, so it appeared my secret was safe with this group.

I was at the coffee table at the back of the room, loading up on caffeine to get me through the next ninety minutes, when Martina Campbell walked to the coffee urns, followed by John Coleman and a tax partner from Kadden Fritz whose name I couldn't recall.

"Kate," Martina said when she noticed me. "I was wondering whether I would see you here. You look great. This break must be agreeing with you."

I wasn't sure how to react to the little snake. The last time I had seen her she was walking down the hall to meet with my biggest client as I packed up my office. I had taken Martina under my wing, trained her. We'd worked late nights together over pizza. Her betrayal, more so than Barry's, had cut me to the quick. However, the last thing I wanted to do was cause a scene. So I joked, "Oh, yes, it's a wonder what more than six hours sleep will do for the complexion, although I'm not sure I'd recommend unemployment as a beauty treatment."

"Well, maybe it's just the break from Barry then," Martina said with a laugh. And when I looked at her uncertainly she added, "Oh, you do know I rejoined Kadden in February, right?"

"No," I said, surprised. "I hadn't heard, although I've been caught up with some, ah, personal matters. I haven't been keeping up with my *Manhattan Law Journal* reading and who's moved where."

"Yeah, well, let's just say Barry and I didn't see eye to eye on many things. Honestly Kate, I don't know how you lasted as long as you did with him. You must be a masochist."

"Maybe I am," I said with a bitter smile.

"You did a good job of shielding the rest of us from him, that's for sure. I had no idea how erratic he was. When he tried to turn me into the next Kate, well, that was never going to work."

I fought to keep my voice steady. "Who's his Kate now?"

"I heard he's trying to groom a fifth year associate he poached from Sterling Harris, a Scarlett somebody or other. I think she's a Yale grad, but since I wasn't at Fowler Sherman very long, I haven't really kept in touch with too many people."

Trying to sound nonchalant, I asked, "What's your deal with Kadden?"

"With all this moving around I've lost two years in terms of partnership track. If all goes according to plan, Kadden will consider me in 2011."

"Well, good luck," I said, not knowing what else to say.

"I have you to thank for that. Because of you I'm miles ahead of where I would otherwise be in terms of my legal writing ability and my structuring knowledge. Even John Coleman has been impressed by my structuring ideas. Not too many partners take the time to train associates as thoroughly as you did. I'll always be grateful."

"Thank you, Martina," I said. This was such a surreal conversation. In all the months I'd imagined what I'd say, or do, to Martina if I ever saw her again, I'd never imagined that I would be thanking her for her compliments. My revenge fantasies generally involved blood and sharp objects.

"I think my time at Fowler Sherman taught me what I don't want," she said. "I'll never again sacrifice my personal life to such a degree, and I'll never surround myself with someone so toxic no matter what carrot they dangle in front of me. Kate, I hope you don't mind me saying this, but wherever you wind up, I hope you don't settle for that type of treatment again either. You're too talented and too decent a person to put up with that."

"It seems you learned in a few months what it has taken me over fifteen years to find out, so I'm not sure I'm so talented after all."

"I know you'll find something, and if I hear of anything I'll certainly let you know. And Kate," she said, turning pink with embarrassment, "if I played any role in what happened to you at Fowler Sherman, I am sorry."

I nodded, acknowledging the apology yet not fully accepting it. "I think they're about to start, we'd better grab our seats."

The rest of the conference flew by. I met many former colleagues and clients and put out feelers for potential jobs. Even if nothing came of them, it felt good to be back in familiar surroundings.

Don Kruger and my dancing partner Paul had mentioned at the ball that they might attend the Symposium. I looked out for Don, and truth be told, Paul as well, however they weren't in any of the seminars I'd signed up for. Still, I brushed my hair and freshened my makeup in the ladies room before I entered the cocktail reception.

He stood across the room, narrow shoulders slightly bent as he loaded up his plate with the free cheese and crackers. Next to him was a petite dark-haired woman, early thirties, with oversized glasses. I was going to have to face him at some point. I straightened my own shoulders and walked over to him.

"Hello, Barry."

"Oh, hello."

"Did you present today?" I asked in a pleasant, neutral tone.

"Yes, I was on the Hot Topics panel, assisted by Scarlett Cutler, our new star associate," he said. Hot Topics was the panel I'd chaired at the conference the previous year, as Barry well knew.

"I'm sorry I missed it. I'm sure it was informative as always."

"Yes."

We stood in uncomfortable silence. Scarlett pretended to receive an important message on her Blackberry. "Will you both excuse me, I need to call the office," she said.

"Of course. It was nice meeting you."

Barry's eyes darted around the room as he looked for his own escape, but I stood in front of him. "What happened last November?"

"What do you mean what happened?" Barry snarled, all pretense at surface pleasantries having evaporated. "The firm needed to make cutbacks. It was nothing personal."

"Nothing personal? We were partners, partners in every sense of the word for fifteen years. I sacrificed everything for the Hedge Funds Group, for you. I was one hundred percent loyal to you, and I gave you no reason, no reason at all, to do what you did. I deserve some type of explanation." I felt my cheeks redden with anger.

"I owe you nothing. You were distracted by your home situation. You were off your game."

"That's bullshit and you know it."

"It wasn't just my decision, it was the Executive Committee's decision as well."

"Oh, please, Barry. Don't insult my intelligence. I know you, and only you, were behind my firing. I've had months to think about it, and do you know why I think you did it? I think you were worried about me being nominated to the Executive Committee. You knew that if I ever got on that committee, you'd lose control of the Hedge Funds Group. I had the support of Ken Shine, support you'd never had. I chaired several important conferences and started to bring in my own clients. You were threatened. But you know what, Barry? The joke is really on you. I would've turned them down. I had no desire to serve on the Executive Committee. I know I did all the grunt work in terms of the work flow and dealing with the associates. I know you got the bulk of the glory and the money, but I didn't care. I was comfortable in my niche. I would've continued making you and your department money until I was ready to retire."

"You're wrong," he said, without conviction.

"I'm right, and you know I'm right. Martina lasted three months. How long do you think this Scarlett will last? A year, maybe two if you're lucky. How many associates have left since bonuses were paid in February? As soon as the economy picks up, I guarantee there'll be a mass exodus. I predict you'll find yourself back on the fifth floor next to the word processing department before you know it."

"And where's *your* office, Kate?"

"I'm still evaluating my options."

"Well, good luck with that. We're done here," Barry said as he walked across the room to the bar. I took a deep breath and tried to slow my racing heart. I heard someone clapping behind me. It was Paul.

I turned around to look at him, his brown eyes filled with compassion and something else I couldn't quite put my finger on. "How much did you hear?"

"Enough. Why don't we get out of here? I happen to have dinner reservations at Le Cirque for eight o'clock, compliments of the LICKs silent auction," he said with a smile. "I would be honored if you would join me."

"Oh, I don't want to intrude if you have prior plans," I said.

"Kate." Paul took a step closer. "I made those reservations hoping I would see you here."

"Oh."

"I promise I won't bite. Please, have dinner with me."

I looked around the room and felt very tired. My confrontation with Barry, although a long time coming, seemed to have sapped my energy. I looked at Paul, who appeared to have taken extra care with his grooming and splashed on a spicy cologne, and I was touched. I smiled. "Sure, Paul. I'd love to go to dinner with you."

He beamed, and I felt like a real jerk for avoiding him these past few weeks. I vowed to myself I would be nothing but fun and upbeat during our dinner. Paul must have had some inkling that he would win me over because a Town Car was waiting outside of the Waldorf to take us the few blocks to Le Cirque. When we arrived at the restaurant, Paul jumped out of the car and walked over to my side and opened the door, holding out his hand. Chivalry was alive and well in midtown Manhattan that night.

Paul guided me into the restaurant, with his hand on my back. Similar to our evening at Oheka Castle, I felt a shiver at such an intimate gesture. We were shown to a prime table and soon an ice cold bottle of pinot grigio appeared.

Paul raised his glass. "Here's to me finally wearing you down."

"I'm glad you did, so let's drink to that." I laughed, clinking my glass with his.

Paul allayed any fears I had about being on my first date in over ten years by keeping the conversation easy and light. There was no discussion of old relationships, careers or anything else that could possibly cause me angst. We discussed restaurants he'd recently been to, his plans to visit his twin sons at their college in San Diego and the renovations to his Centre Island home.

"You have a home on Centre Island?" I asked.

"Yes, I bought it several years ago as a weekend home. I wanted something on the water, and the Hamptons aren't exactly my scene."

"Okay, you may think this is a strange question, is your house anywhere near Billy Jones's house?"

"Yeah, it's two houses down."

"Oh my God! Do you know him?"

"Of course I know him--it's a fairly small community."

"Are you like, friends?"

"Well, we don't hang out or anything. I know him well enough to wave to him. To tell you the truth, he's not exactly my favorite neighbor. He's always tooling around on his obnoxious motorcycles. I mean, come on, how old is he anyway?" Paul said, shaking his head.

"It's not like he's having a mid-life crisis or anything. He's been riding motorcycles for years."

"You wouldn't think it was quite so cool if a roaring motorcycle woke you up at three in the morning," Paul said. "Hey, wait a second, why do you know so much about him? Did you date him or something?"

"Date him? Me? Oh my God, you've got to be kidding."

He chuckled. "Oh, you're a fan, aren't you? Are you president of his fan club?"

"Okay, I admit it. I am a member of his fan club. But I'm not like a stalker or anything."

"Hey, you're not just using me to get to Billy, are you?" he teased.

"Of course not."

"If you play your cards right, Ms. Ryan, I may wrangle an autograph for you."

"Could you really?" I asked.

"Of course not. We all try and pretend we're not even aware he's a celebrity. I was invited to the Centre Island Conservation Annual Dinner, and he often makes an appearance. It's in two weeks. Perhaps you'd like to accompany me?"

"Oh, I would love to!"

"So if I call you," he said with a smile, "you'll answer the phone next time."

I had the decency to flush with embarrassment. "Listen, Paul, I'm sorry. It was just a bad time for me."

He put his hand over mine. "I was only teasing. I'm happy to spend time with you tonight. No pressure, I promise."

After our coffee, we left Le Cirque and the Town Car was waiting out front.

"I took the train in. You can drop me at Penn Station," I said to the driver when we got settled in the car.

"Don't be silly. It's too late for you to take the train now. The car will take you home." Paul then said to the driver, "Two stops. 25 East 85th, and the second stop is out on Long Island."

"No really, Paul, I'll be fine on the train."

"Another word out of you, and I'll insist you stay at my place." And with that he moved closer to me in the backseat and took my hand. He leaned toward me and gave me a soft kiss. Almost against my will, I started to kiss him back, and during the fifteen minute drive to his apartment our kisses became deeper and more urgent. He'd almost made it to second base when the car stopped.

"Kate," he said in a deep husky voice, "I would love nothing better than to take you upstairs, but I want to do this right. Can I call you tomorrow?"

"Of course," I said with a mixture of disappointment and relief.

"Good night."

"Good night, Paul, and thanks. Thanks for everything."

Chapter 13

The next two weeks passed without too much incident. The remaining *Gold Coast Wives* episodes aired, including a heavily edited version of the "bonus" episode shot at Wolf Lodge Casino. And of course the ratings continued to grow. If I'd ever left my house I'm sure I would've been assaulted with all sorts of viewers and their varied opinions. However, I kept my forays from my house on Trafalgar Court to a minimum. The only noteworthy thing that happened was after the finale aired and people heard Rachel call us a bunch of Irish drunks, my Uncle Danny, the sitting president of the Nassau County Ancient Order of Hibernians, started a letter writing campaign against Finley's Fine Furnishings. The AOH had even taken out ads in several local town newspapers calling for a boycott until Finley's issued a public apology. Danny's wife, my very excitable Aunt Agnes, called me in a tizzy and told me she was never shopping at Finley's again. Given Agnes had last bought a piece of furniture in 1992, I didn't think that was much of a threat. However, when Danny and his cronies scheduled a rally outside of Finley's during their Memorial Day sale, David Finley called me.

"Kate," David said in a low courteous voice, "I'm sorry to bother you at home. I don't know if you're aware an Irish group is boycotting my store and causing me all kinds of headaches."

"Yes, I heard something to that effect."

"Well, you wouldn't happen to be a member of this Hibernation club, would you?"

"I'm not a member, no," I said, "but my father and uncles are members."

"I'm sorry to ask this, but if there's anything you could do to help stop this, I would really appreciate it. The economy's been tough enough, and I don't need negative publicity on top of it. I could kill Rachel for what she said, but you know yourself, many stupid things were said in the heat of the moment during that damn show. Believe me, Rachel may be a bit hot-headed, but she's not prejudiced."

That was debatable. However, David had never been anything but decent to me. It seemed unfair that the business he had worked so hard to build was to be yet another casualty of the *Gold Coast Wives* mess.

"Look, the Hibernians are not going to stop until they get some kind of public apology. Maybe you could have Channel 45 tape an apology they can air on *Long Island Today*. Then if you meet with the President of the AOH, and maybe hand him a gift voucher--I know their meeting rooms could always do with a coat of paint and new curtains--I think we can make this thing go away."

"Oh, that would be great. I am so grateful, and I'm sorry if Rachel's words insulted you and your family in any way."

I felt bad this poor man had to apologize for his lunatic of a wife, so I took the high road. "I understand. I'll check with the Hibernians and get back to you."

Uncle Danny and his AOH friends eventually accepted David's proposal, and the matter was laid to rest. The last thing I wanted was for any member of my family to make a public spectacle of themselves. I had done quite enough in that department.

Paul called me almost daily. We had been unable to meet because Don's firm, DTK Advisors, was undergoing an SEC exam. It seemed the SEC had uncovered something. Paul couldn't tell me what it was and, to tell the truth, I really didn't want to know. Helping Don out of this SEC mess was taking up all of Paul's free time. But he had called in the morning to confirm we were still on for the Centre Island Conservation Annual Dinner that evening.

Even though Paul had already seen me in the green empire-waisted cocktail dress I'd worn to Pamela's book launch, I decided to wear it again. It was the most appropriate dress in my closet, and I couldn't face hitting the mall and being inundated with *Gold Coast Wives* questions. I hoped the Centre Island crowd was sophisticated enough to have missed the *Gold Coast Wives* mania that had seemed to afflict the rest of the Island. But truth be told, I was so excited to see Paul again that a few obnoxious questions from fans seemed a small price to pay. Plus, I might be able to see Billy Jones. I hoped he'd leave his embryonic wife at home.

Despite my mother's immersion in her memoir, she agreed to watch Lucy for the evening. My parents arrived at my house around five to give me a chance to get ready.

As my mother served Lucy the roast beef and mashed potatoes she'd brought with her, I showered. I took great care with my hair and makeup, and even wore the red lipstick Chris had given me for the finale, which Deirdre liked to call my *fuck me* lipstick. Not that I wanted things to go that far this evening--at least I didn't *think* I wanted things to go that far.

When I went downstairs, Lucy was happily sitting on my father's lap, snapping barrettes onto his few remaining strands of hair while they watched Bill O'Reilly. My mother was scrolling through her manuscript and sipping tea.

"Is it done?" I asked.

"Yes, finally. I'm just putting the finishing touches on it."

"Congratulations. Are you pleased with it?"

"It's different from anything I've ever written before, obviously. I think I like it, though."

"Oh, good. I can't wait to read it."

"I don't want anyone to read it until my editor reads it first," my mother said, looking embarrassed.

"Your Heartland editor?"

"No, one of Heartland's sister companies, Cornice Publishing, is interested and they assigned me a new editor."

"Oh, Mom, what fantastic news!"

"Not so fast, she might hate the final manuscript. She liked the first thirty pages, though."

"I'm sure she'll love the whole thing."

"Oh, and the best thing is, if it does get published, it will be under my own name, Grace Griffin," she said with pride.

"That's fantastic. I'll bet Heartland is sorry they let you go now."

"Oh, didn't I tell you? Heartland didn't let me go. Thanks to my exposure on *Gold Coast Wives*, my Long Island sales have shot through the roof! They're going to put more money in promoting *A Pocketful of Gold* nationwide. They still want me to write more Penelope La Montagne books!"

"At least something good has come out of this whole fiasco."

"Did Deirdre tell you about her cards?" Grace asked. "She's received close to five hundred orders already."

"I've been lying low lately and haven't spoken to her. So she's not devastated about how she was portrayed on the finale and the Wolf Lodge episode?"

"She wasn't happy, of course, but I think that slutty niece and Pamela came off much worse. What was with her strange Halloween costumes anyway? Leather bras, for goodness sake. Not very classy if you ask me. And don't even get me started about Rachel. She's a total rip altogether."

"Yeah, tell me about it. Even Aunt Agnes wanted to have a go at her," I said with a laugh.

"Honestly, Agnes and Danny have no sense of proportion. Those two wanted your father and me to march around holding a banner, if you can believe it," she huffed. "As if I don't have enough to do."

I laughed at the thought of my mother protesting anything--she wasn't much of a joiner. "Overall, what did you *really* think of the show?"

"Honestly, I didn't like the way they portrayed you as being so insecure all the time. In fairness, you were going through a hard time. Still are, I suppose. What I don't understand is if you knew you were going to be on camera, why on earth didn't you get to those events on time? Pamela was right about that--the other Wives shouldn't have had to wait around for you."

"I was on time," I protested. "They just taped it to make it look like I was late."

"Oh, and what were you doing with that massage fella?"

"Nothing went on."

"It sure looked like something went on," she said, eyeing me with suspicion. "It's over now anyway, thank God."

"Yes, thank God."

"What's the story with this Paul character?"

"There's no story, Mom, honest. I like him, we have a nice time together. He asked me to go to this dinner, and since I've been a shut-in the last few weeks, I said I'd go."

"Just be careful," she said looking down at her computer screen. I think my mother was a little embarrassed to be having this type of conversation with me, her forty-two-year old daughter whom she thought she'd married off years ago.

"Don't worry," I said. "I will."

Twenty minutes later Paul arrived and after he made the obligatory small talk with the parents, we were off. It felt a little bit like we were going to the prom--I almost thought my father was going to warn Paul to have me home by eleven.

I had half expected Paul to arrive in a zippy red convertible, which seemed to me what a fiftyish hedge fund honcho should drive. However, he arrived in a well-worn, brown pick-up truck. We sat together in comfortable silence listening to some classic rock during the twenty-five minute ride to Centre Island.

Paul stopped in front of a 1920s vintage mansion with stunning views of Oyster Bay. Ever the gentleman, he walked to my side of the truck and opened my door. We walked up the stone walkway. A tall silver-haired gentleman of about sixty-five, our host for the evening, greeted us warmly and led us to the dining room where a raw bar had been set up. Along with twenty other couples, we availed ourselves of the cold lobster and oysters.

"Paul, I thought this was going to be a big dinner, I didn't realize it was going to be such a small group. I thought the purpose was to raise money."

"There are some pretty deep pockets here, but the projects the Committee works on are usually fairly small in scale. I think this year they want to add new lights around the marina on the east side of the island. It's a chance for neighbors to get together as much as anything else. You're not sorry you came, are you?" he asked. He looked a little anxious.

"Of course not," I assured him.

"Good, because I've been missing you since that night at Le Cirque."

"Me too," I said, willing my cheeks not to blush.

"I hope we're not interrupting," said a tall blond woman, around mid-forties, who sat down next to me and was accompanied by another blonde wearing a pair of silver owl earrings.

"Carol, Lorraine, how are you?" Paul asked.

"Oh, fine. Sorry, Paul, we didn't stop by to talk to you. We wanted to talk to your lovely companion. You're Kate from *Gold Coast Wives*, aren't you?"

"Would you believe me if I said I had an evil twin?"

"I knew it," said the blonde with the owl earrings. "My girlfriends and I are completely addicted. I even ordered some of your friend's earrings!"

"I see that. The owls look wonderful on you."

"Tell me, Kate, did your sister break up with Gordon?" Carol asked.

I laughed. "No, no. Although he did spend some time in the doghouse."

"He is so cute. I can't imagine how you can sit across the Thanksgiving table from Gordon without completely attacking him!"

"My sister has a mean right hook. Besides, I've known him since he was eighteen--he's like a brother to me." Paul, having overdosed on the *Gold Coast Wives* thing, left to freshen our drinks.

"Well, you didn't do so bad yourself, Kate," Carol said as soon as Paul left. "Paul is the number one eligible bachelor here on Centre Island. Unfortunately, he's good friends with my ex-husband."

"And I'm good friends with Paul's ex-wife," said Lorraine.

"Paul is sweet. We're just friends, though," I said with a blush.

"Honey, we all saw you dance," Lorraine said. "If you're not more than friends now, you will be soon. Oh speak of the devil. Paul, we were telling Kate how much we liked your dancing."

"I had a wonderful partner," Paul said as I tried not to laugh.

Lorraine and Carol soon went off to circulate, and a few more women asked various show-related questions. They were all so sweet that I didn't have the heart to brush them off. After a dinner of Dover sole, Paul said, "I think I've subjected you to enough scrutiny tonight. Would you like to go back to my house and have coffee?"

Trying not to sound too disappointed, I said, "I guess Billy's a no show, huh?"

"Well, we could wait around and see if he turns up for dessert."

"No, no, I'd love to see your house," I said with forced enthusiasm. Much as I wanted to see Paul's house, I had been looking forward to meeting Billy again, and actually being able to remember it. Oh well, another dream dashed.

As we thanked our hosts, Carol gave me a wink as if to say, "I know why you're leaving early." I just smiled in return.

Paul lived on the other side of the island, facing Lloyd Neck, and we drove there in less than ten minutes. His house was an imposing stone Tudor, not unlike Don and Pamela's, except rather than surrounded by horse paddocks, Paul's had expansive views of the Long Island Sound.

As we walked through the doorway, I noticed the house was decorated with those small touches that indicated a woman had lived here in the not-so-distant past. Not wanting to break the mood by asking any questions, I told Paul that he had a beautiful home. We entered his gleaming chef's kitchen to start the coffee. He made the coffee while I set up the cups and sugar on a tray, our movements in synch like an old married couple. Paul carried the tray into the living room. Because it was a warm evening, he opened the French doors to the deck. The quiet lapping of the Long Island Sound filled the room.

Paul hit a few buttons on one of his remotes, and the soft sounds of jazz surrounded us. I tucked myself into a corner of the soft leather couch and held my steaming cup of coffee. Paul, I suppose not wanting to seem too forward, sat across the room in a large brown leather chair.

"Listen, I have to ask this. Why on earth have you been anxious to see me again? According to Carol and Lorraine, you're quite the catch around here. Why pursue a semi-divorced, unemployed, reality TV freak?"

"Wow, Kate, don't beat around the bush."

"No, I'm curious. You're wealthy, single, smart, funny. You could go out with anyone. Why me?"

"And handsome. You forgot handsome," Paul said with a smile.

"That goes without saying."

He paused for a moment. "I don't know, really. I suppose you caught my attention. I saw you standing there at the yacht club in that amazing green dress, checking your watch every few minutes. You were obviously bored out of your mind and didn't care who knew it. Plus, I'd heard how you had driven Pamela nuts. I figured if you could make old Pammy that crazy, you must be my kind of gal."

"Your kind of gal, huh?" I laughed.

Paul moved over and sat next to me on the couch. "Yeah, my kind of gal." He put his arms around me and gave me a long, deep kiss. "I've been waiting to do that all night," he said. I kissed him back. Paul's kisses became deeper and more urgent. I felt his hands slide down my body, which felt good. Real good. Next, I felt his hand slip beneath my dress and climb up my leg. I froze. I was wearing a rubbery body shaper Chris had promised was even stronger than Spanx, and while the body shaper did a great job keeping everything in its place, it didn't exactly scream *sexy*. God, why hadn't I prepared better for this?

Paul must have assumed I stopped him because I was shy, not because I was encased in rubber and looked like an overstuffed sausage. The kissing continued, and I believe he was enjoying it as much as I was. I may be a size fourteen--okay sixteen--but ever since I had broken out of my *good girl* shell in college, I've been a hell of a kisser. My nose started to twitch in response to his spicy cologne--thank God I suppressed my sneeze. Making out with non-husbands was tricky.

Paul stroked my breasts, and I ran my hand through his coarse salt and pepper hair, which he seemed to like and take as encouragement. His hand slipped below the neckline of my dress and over my triple-strength minimizer bra, also not exactly the sexiest garment. But at this point things were getting pretty heated, and I felt like I had to throw him some type of bone--we weren't thirteen after all. Paul pushed me back down on the couch and was somehow able to release my left breast from the vise grip of the minimizer bra. He began to softly kiss my nipple. I then offered up the right breast which he laid bare, kissing that nipple also. His kisses became more insistent, and he began to suck and almost nibble on my breasts. I hadn't been touched by a man in so long, and it felt amazing. I started to moan and wiggle out of my green dress when the phone rang.

"Ignore it," I said in a husky voice.

"Are you kidding? Of course I'm going to ignore it, now that I have you where I want you." He helped me out of my dress and didn't even seem to notice the body shaper when I heard a woman's voice boom from his answering machine in the kitchen.

"Paul! Paul, please answer the phone if you're there. I've been trying to reach you all night. I think your cell's turned off. Don's been arrested for insider trading. The police and the FBI were here this afternoon. Don told me to get in touch with you and hand you a file. He wants you to explain it to his lawyers. Please, Paul," she sobbed, "I'm losing my mind here. You have to call me back!"

If anyone was going to ruin the first sex I'd had in over six months, it would have to be Pamela Kruger.

Paul just looked at me. I put my clothes back on, the neckline of my green dress now stretched out of shape. While Paul called Pamela back, I went to the bathroom to put myself back together before I had to face my parents.

We didn't say much on the drive back to my house. As we turned onto Trafalgar Court, I broke the silence. "My former litigation partner at Fowler Sherman, Carlton Landry, is one of the top white-collar specialists in the city. Let me know if you'd like an introduction."

"Oh, Don's already got a lawyer."

"Not for Don," I said, looking into his brown eyes. "For you."

* * * *

The next day I couldn't get in touch with Paul, but I did leave Carlton Landry's phone number on his answering machine. I also called Carlton and told him he should expect a call from Paul. It was clear to me brotherly love wasn't the only reason Paul was involved in Don's SEC investigation, but I wasn't his lawyer. I was only his sort-of girlfriend. It wasn't my place to fix this problem, and given my own situation, I wasn't sure how much I wanted to get involved. I liked Paul well enough--okay, I liked him a lot. But that was when I thought he was an attractive, attentive suitor with an appreciation for my cleavage. If he was involved in insider trading...well then, let's just say I hadn't signed up for conjugal visits at Sing-Sing.

While Lucy was at nursery school, I caught up on some bills. My little *Gold Coast Wives* nest egg, even with the extra payments I'd received for the Wolf Lodge episode, was depleting at a rapid rate, and my next fifteen-thousand, four hundred dollar semi-annual property tax installment would take another big chunk out of it in June. I hadn't heard from Kyle Madden of Handler Associates in some time, so I called him. Not surprisingly, no suitable partnership level positions had come up. Kyle sounded shocked when I said I was willing to relocate anywhere in the country and was also open to short-term consulting positions. Beggars can't be choosers.

I also checked in with Karen Rice to see how my abandonment petition was going. She said things were progressing. If we could get hold of Jim and file a more normal divorce petition, it would simplify things. Ever the optimist, I sent *NYJimmy66* yet another email, asking him to get in touch directly with my lawyer if he didn't want to talk to me. Since I had started dating--even with a potential felon--I wanted my marital status to be settled. For legal and for moral reasons.

About a half hour before I had to pick up Lucy from school, I answered the phone to hear Angela's screeching voice on the other end. "Are you sitting down? I have the most amazing news!"

"You're adding giraffes to your jewelry line?"

"Not a bad idea, but no, that's not why I'm calling. Channel 45 sold its rights to *Gold Coast Wives* to Encore. We're going national, baby!"

"You're kidding me, right? This is your idea of a joke."

"No joke, Kit Kat. We're going to be available in all fifty states!"

"How could this happen?"

"Ratings, baby, ratings. The show's ratings for both men and women between the ages of twenty five and forty five were through the roof. Do you know that even college boys watch the show?"

"You don't say."

"Do you know what this will mean for Angela Rosetti Fine Jewelry? Sky's the limit!"

"Do you know what this will mean for Kate Ryan? People in all fifty states will be able to look at my fat ass as I'm shown cleaning my fridge. Or better yet, they can see me in HD as my face erupts in hives. Or they can--"

"Enough already," Angela interrupted. "You're bringing me down. This is a good thing, Kate. A very good thing"

"It may be good for you. It's not so good for me."

"Fine, be that way. I'm calling Deirdre. I bet she'll be happy about the news." And with that, Angela hung up.

If I found it difficult to find a job now, what would it be like when people really started to watch the show?

That night, after I put Lucy to bed, I took a copy of my *Gold Coast Wives* contract along with a pen and a large yellow legal pad into the great room where I made myself comfortable on one of Rachel's yellow chairs.

Putting my lawyer's hat on, I read the contract and took careful notes. Not quite believing what I had just read, I sent an email to Glenn Meyers.

Glenn,

I survived the Gold Coast Wives taping. Now my worst nightmare has come true. Apparently Channel 45 has sold the rights to Encore, a nationwide cable channel. Rather than jumping out a window, I read through the contract to see if there was any way I could block this transaction. Although I didn't see anything that would require my consent to the sale, I did read several provisions I would like to discuss with you. They are as follows:

Schedule 1, Section 2-b: Participant will receive an additional payment equal to five percent of revenues generated from every subsequent airing of the Episodes.

Schedule 1, Section 2-b: Upon the sale of the Show to any third party Participant will receive a one-time payment equal to ten percent of the Purchase Price.

Schedule 2, Section 4-b: Participant will receive a royalty payment equal to two percent for any and all products licensed by Channel 45 or any Subsequent Purchaser or any other party if such products contain the name "Gold Coast," "Gold Coast Wives," or refer in any respect to such names or the name of the Participant.

If I'm reading these provisions correctly, it looks like I may be entitled to some additional payments. I'm available anytime tomorrow to discuss.

Thanks,

Kate

With any luck, that tax bill would be less of a problem.

The next morning at eleven, Glenn called me with one of his litigation partners.

"Kate, is now a good time to talk?"

"Sure, I don't have to pick up Lucy for another hour."

"Good. I discussed your contract with my partner Eliot Hansen who is on the phone with us."

"Did I read your riders correctly then?" I asked.

"You sure did. You are definitely entitled to more payments, and if the show proves successful in syndication, a lot more."

"Oh my God. That's fantastic!"

"Since we weren't notified of the sale to Encore, we suspect upper management of both Channel 45 and Encore may be unaware of your contract's riders. I suspected at the time that the woman who coordinated the contract didn't seem too sophisticated."

"Yeah, Channel 45 is a bit of a Mickey Mouse operation all right."

"We should be prepared for a fight. It's doubtful Encore will simply write you a check, since they probably know about your reduced circumstances. I expect that they'll either try to intimidate you by filing numerous motions, or they'll offer you a low ball settlement offer," Eliot said.

"What do you suggest I do?"

"We've discussed it with our partners, and they agreed if we can get this in front of a judge or an arbitrator, you'll eventually be successful. Kate. We've agreed to forgo our fees until this is resolved, which is not something we typically do," Glenn said.

"Oh, Glenn, thank you."

"Glenn and I have contacted Encore's general counsel."

"Okay, let me know if you need anything else," I said.

"We will. Keep your fingers crossed," Glenn said.

To add to my emotional roller coaster, Paul called later that afternoon, during Lucy's nap. He was subdued and very unlike the relaxed man who had whisked me off to Le Cirque.

"I'm sorry I've been out of touch. I've been helping Pamela access some of Don's private accounts to come up with his bail."

"He's out of jail?"

"Yes. He got out yesterday."

"Oh good. That must be a relief."

"It is. I was glad to help. Pamela doesn't have the first clue about their finances."

"She's lucky you were there to help," I said. "I hope she appreciates all you've done."

"She's so strung out, I don't think she has any idea of what I did, but that's fine. I did it for Don, not her. The only tricky thing now is that your friend Carlton has advised I keep my distance from Don. He's the closest thing I have to a brother--I don't know how I can abandon him."

"Don's a sophisticated guy. I'm sure he'll understand that you're operating under advice of counsel."

"I don't know. I think this Carlton guy's being too cautious. After all I wasn't even aware of what--"

"Stop right there, Paul," I said, interrupting him mid-sentence. "Please don't say anything else. I'm sure Carlton has advised you not to discuss the case with anyone."

"Well, yes. I'm sure he didn't mean you. Attorney-client privilege and all that."

"Paul, I'm a lawyer, but I'm not your lawyer. There's no attorney-client privilege here, and as far as I'm aware, there's no such thing as a girlfriend privilege."

"So," Paul said, the smile creeping back into his voice, "is that what you are?"

"Oh, I, uh, didn't mean girlfriend, girlfriend. I just, uh, you know," I sputtered, "I just meant, like a friend."

"A friend who is an amazing kisser, you mean? Are you sure there's no privilege for that?"

I laughed. "Not that they covered in law school."

"What about a privilege for beautiful breasts?" Paul asked, his voice slightly hoarse and very sexy. "Is there a beautiful breast privilege?"

"No," I said, my own voice becoming lower, "I don't remember that one either." Oh my God, were we about to have phone sex? Was this what phone sex even was? And was I really the type of girl to have phone sex with semi-strangers? At the rate I was going I'd have a web cam next.

"What about a privilege for..."

Our privileged phone sex conversation went on for a half hour. And yes, I did feel a little dirty afterward.

* * * *

Glenn called the next day to give me an update. Apparently the brass at Channel 45 and Encore had no idea my contract was anything other than the typical one-sided boiler plate laden contract common in reality TV land. Elaine kept fairly incomplete files, and couldn't even find all the pages to my contract. Glenn hand messengered the complete notarized copies of my contract to both channels the day before and also delivered a notice to each of them demanding an accounting of the purchase price paid by Encore and the proposed broadcast schedule. Best case scenario, we could expect a response sometime the next week. Until this matter was resolved, Glenn cautioned me to avoid the other cast members and anyone else associated with Channel 45, including Angela and Chris.

I wasn't allowed to see Angela, Paul had a meeting with Carlton Landry and an SEC examiner, Deirdre was in school and my mother had a meeting with her new editor. I had a play date scheduled with the dance school yummies for the next day, so Lucy and I were at loose ends. It was a beautiful May morning, and I decided to do the unthinkable by driving to my mother-in-law Peg's house in East Moriches.

The previous day my mother had given me an earful. Apparently Uncle Sean and Peg had met my parents for dinner, and Peg must have taken a personality pill or something because, according to my mother, she was quite pleasant. Uncle Sean must have had a good effect on her. Anyway, Peg mentioned to my mother that she hadn't seen Lucy in months and felt she lost both her son and her granddaughter. Since my parents saw Lucy at least twice a week, my mother felt a bit guilty and decided her good deed for the year was to convince me to take Lucy out east.

Much as it pained me to admit it, my mother had a point. I wasn't deliberately keeping Lucy from Peg all these months--I hadn't been in any shape to subject myself to her underhanded criticism and incessant whining. I also couldn't surround myself with anyone or anything that reminded me of Jim. However, the past few weeks with Paul had restored some of my confidence. And my wounds from Jim, while still painful, were not quite as raw.

With the hope this trip would somehow grant me an extra helping of good karma, I packed bathing suits, beach towels, sun screen and last year's ragged beach toys and headed east on the L.I.E. About an hour later, I pulled up to Peg's clapboard Victorian and saw my Uncle Sean watering a bed of flowers that he must have planted. Peg wasn't much of a green thumb and her garden, although it had stunning views of Moriches Bay, had been rather bland in the past. Sean seemed to be having an impact on Peg's garden as well as her disposition.

"My two favorite ladies!" Uncle Sean shouted over the roar of the hose, as if our little visit wasn't something out of the ordinary. "Peg will be delighted. Go on in the house, I'll be in in a minute. I just want these day lilies to get a good soaking."

With a certain amount of trepidation, I opened Peg's creaky front door.

"Sean, sweetheart, do you want white or whole wheat?"

"Sorry, Peg, it's just us. Kate and Lucy," I called out.

I heard a clatter, as if she dropped some silverware, and then I heard Peg's tiny feet run along the home's old floorboards.

"Oh, oh, Kate. Come in, come in," she said, holding back as if uncertain whether she should attempt a hug.

"Peg." I stepped forward and gave her a small hug. "You look wonderful." It was true, I hadn't remembered ever seeing Peg look so good. Her usual pallor was replaced by red, almost rosy cheeks, a result I suspect of my Uncle Sean's fondness for long walks. Her steel gray helmet of tight curls, maintained by her bi-weekly beauty parlor appointments, had been replaced by a softer, longer pageboy, and it suited her.

"Thank you, dear." Dear? "You're looking very well yourself. And this little lady, she's gorgeous. She's the very image of you." Peg bent down to Lucy's level. "Would you like some chocolate milk? I seem to remember you're a great fan of chocolate milk."

"Yes, miss, I would like some milk." Lucy gave her grandmother a shy smile.

"You can call me Granny Peg, child. Now come along with me." Peg took Lucy's hand and guided her to the adjoining room.

I carried my bag into Peg's living room which was adorned with many pictures of her late husband, her children and fourteen grandchildren. I caught a glimpse of my own wedding portrait, which I had since banished to my basement. I also saw some newer pictures: one of Sean and Peg dancing at the Irish-American Hall in Mineola, a group portrait of the Griffins taken at my Uncle Danny's sixtieth birthday party and, most surprising of all, a picture of Sean and Peg on what could only be a Caribbean cruise. Would wonders never cease?

I was still looking at Peg's pictures when my Uncle Sean came in.

"I see you made the wall," I said, pointing to the new pictures. "How on earth did you convince Peg to go on a cruise? Jim and I have been begging her to go on one for years."

"I didn't have to convince her--it was her idea," he said with a twinkle in his eye.

I laughed. "After you planted the seed, I imagine. Anyway, you both seem happy."

"Yes, I was very lucky that Peg agreed to go out with me." Did he really think there were other suitors banging down her door? Oh, well, ignorance is bliss I supposed. "This visit will do Peg a world of good. Thank you for coming. I know it's probably not easy being back here."

"It's fine, really. It's much easier than I thought it would be." I glanced at Jim's Holy Communion picture. "Plus, it was the right thing to do. I'm sorry now I left it so late."

"You're here now, that's what counts." Sean squeezed my arm. "Let's go into the kitchen, I think Peg's making tuna sandwiches for lunch."

When we entered the kitchen, Lucy and Peg were the best of friends. Peg had let Lucy set the table, and Lucy was quite proud of herself. We ate a simple lunch of tuna fish sandwiches and potato chips. It was calm and free of the underlying tension that had marred many of the meals I'd previously shared with Peg at this table. Maybe what Peg needed all this time was a man of her own to fuss over and make tuna fish sandwiches for. Maybe then she wouldn't have leaned so much on her children.

After lunch, Sean took Lucy down by the dock at the end of Peg's property to see if his crab trap had caught anything.

"It's a beautiful day, Kate," Peg said. "Why don't I pour us some iced tea and we can sit on the porch."

"Sounds great."

After we'd settled ourselves on Peg's ancient white wicker chairs, Peg said "Jim finally called last week."

"Oh?"

"Yes, and Maura heard from him yesterday. At least we know he's in one piece."

"I haven't spoken to him since before Christmas, though it wasn't for lack of trying on my part," I said, not even trying to hide my bitterness.

"I know, Kate, I know." She patted my hand, trying to comfort me in her small way. Who was this woman? "He mentioned that you want a divorce."

"Yes. He left seven months ago, and I need some resolution. Did he say anything else about the divorce?"

"No, only that he was surprised."

"Is he out of his mind? How could he possibly be surprised?" I said, my voicing getting higher with each word.

"I don't know, I didn't ask him because I didn't want to push him too hard in case he hung up on me. I'll tell you this, Kate, I am not proud of my son. I didn't think I raised the kind of man who would run off and leave his family. I'm sorry you've had to go through this. I don't know how you're holding up as well as you are."

In all the years I'd known Peg, I'd never heard her say a word against Jim, and she'd never once said a nice thing to me. This was all a bit much to take in.

"I'm not sure that I'm holding up that well, to be quite honest. Lucy and I are surviving and still have a roof over our heads."

"No thanks to my son, I know." Peg's face fell, and I noticed she looked every one of her seventy two years.

Sean and Lucy soon returned. Lucy had gathered two bouquets of dandelions for me and Peg, who started to get teary. "Thanks, sweetheart," she said to Lucy, looking over her head at me.

With hugs, kisses and promises to return soon, Lucy and I left East Moriches for our hour long drive back to Huntington Bay. I thought of all the times I had driven this route with Jim, my head often caught in the vise-like grip of a tension headache. This time, with Lucy snoring in her booster seat and Norah Jones crooning on the car stereo, I felt nothing but calm.

* * * *

Paul and I spoke several times during the week. Unfortunately, we were unable to meet because he often had daily meetings in the city with his lawyers and the SEC. Besides, Lucy had come down with a bad ear infection, so I didn't feel right leaving her with a baby sitter while Mommy got her groove on. Paul and I did, however, burn up the phone lines, to put it mildly.

The following week, Glenn asked me to meet him at an office building on Avenue of the Americas near 50th Street. Channel 45 and Encore had refused to provide the accounting directly to Glenn, electing to invoke the contract's arbitration clause instead. Glenn, Eliot and I were to meet with Channel 45 and Encore and their respective lawyers at the offices of an approved arbitrator.

Our assigned arbitrator was Chuck Belkner. Eliot said he was a tough old bird but was not known for capricious decisions. Given the arbitrators we could have drawn, Eliot was pleased overall to have been assigned Belkner.

The only member of Channel 45's three person team whom I recognized was Elaine. I gave her a wide smile which she refused to acknowledge. The Encore representatives, a man and woman both in their late forties perhaps, were quite cordial and shook my hand. We sat around a gleaming conference room table and made small talk as we waited for Mr. Belkner's arrival.

Ten minutes later, in a baggy, rumpled gray suit and a coffee-stained tie, Chuck Belkner entered the room trailed by an older woman holding a stack of documents.

"Good morning," he growled. "I have this room booked for the next two hours. However, based on my review of the disputed contract, I don't see why we can't be out of here sooner. Now, who is here from Meyers and Finkel?" Glenn and Eliot raised their hands. Chuck turned his steely gaze to me and said, "And you're Kate Ryan?" I simply nodded. He then looked to the other side of the table. "I'm going to hear from them first, okay?" Elaine glared but the older man with wire glasses, who looked like the head lawyer, agreed that was fine. "All right, we'll hear from Ms. Ryan's counsel. You have the floor, gentlemen."

Glenn walked the arbitrator through the time line of the negotiations of the contract with Channel 45. He pulled out copies of emails sent to Elaine and copies of his time sheets, describing every interaction with Channel

45. He provided a quick summary of the terms of the riders outlining my obligations under the contract and the disputed pay out terms. Eliot outlined the demand for an accounting he sent to Channel 45 and Encore on my behalf.

Belkner simply nodded during my lawyers' presentation. He turned to the group on the other side of the conference table and asked which one of them was Elaine.

Elaine, whose face had turned tomato red with temper, snapped, "I am."

"All right, could someone from Channel 45 explain for us the negotiations of the contract?" Belkner asked.

A rather nondescript man with a bad comb-over raised his hand. "I'm Bill Webster from Channel 45 legal. Ms. Rogers handled the negotiations."

"Fine," Mr. Belkner said. "Ms. Rogers, proceed."

"I'd be happy to. Ms. Ryan told me she sent the contract to her lawyer. I don't remember all those emails. I had expected Ms. Ryan's lawyer to review the contract and explain it to her. She's supposed to be a lawyer herself, so I don't understand why she needed another lawyer. Anyway, when I received the contract, I signed it and had it notarized."

"How would you characterize the negotiations of the riders?" Belkner asked.

"I don't know what you're talking about. The contract came back, with Kate's name filled in and the date. And then I signed it."

"You didn't discuss the riders with Ms. Ryan or her attorney?" Belkner asked.

"No. I was under a tight deadline to start filming."

"Did you even read the riders, Ms. Rogers?"

"I told you I was busy. I didn't have time for all that stupid paperwork." The two Encore execs exchanged a look. Poor Mr. Webster looked like he wanted to hide under the table.

"Did your internal lawyers review the riders?"

"Oh, those guys just slow things up. Plus, Bill Webster provided the form I sent to Ms. Ryan. He left the contract execution to me."

"And you didn't alert Mr. Webster to the fact there were amendments made to the contract?"

Elaine looked at me. "You never told me that the contract was amended."

"Ms. Ryan," Mr. Belkner said turning to me, "what was your involvement in the negotiations?"

"None. I'm a hedge fund lawyer, and I don't know entertainment law. I hired Mr. Meyers's firm because they are experts in the area."

"So you didn't discuss the contract with Ms. Rogers?"

"Other than to tell her I signed it, no."

"Do you generally sign documents without reading them, Ms. Rogers?" Mr. Belkner growled.

"Um, ah, no."

"You did in this case, correct? And you didn't send it to anyone else to review and explain it to you, even though it sounds like you have internal legal counsel available to you. Do I have that right?"

"Yes," Elaine said with a small defeated sigh.

"And now you expect me to set aside this contract because you didn't have time to read it before you signed it?" Belkner shouted. He took a deep breath before continuing. "I see no compelling reason why we should not respect the four corners of this document. Channel 45 and Encore will provide the requested accounting to Ms. Ryan and her counsel within five business days, with the required payments to date to follow within ten business days. Is there anything else to discuss here?"

One of the Encore lawyers handed Mr. Belkner and Glenn a document, and said, "Encore was not provided with copies of the riders prior to purchasing the rights to *Gold Coast Wives*, but that is something we will handle outside of this arbitration," he said, looking directly at Elaine while she squirmed in her chair. "However, we would like Ms. Ryan and her attorneys to consider this settlement contract we've drafted. The payout terms under Ms. Ryan's current contract are not standard for Encore and create accounting difficulties."

Glenn looked at Mr. Belkner. "Is there a separate conference room we could use?"

"Helen," he said to his assistant who had been diligently taking the minutes of the arbitration, "please show them to Conference Room C."

Glenn, Eliot and I followed Helen to a smaller conference room. The three of us wordlessly sat at the table and read the contract.

My heart raced as I read through the contract. I looked up to see Glenn's big grin.

"Am I reading this correctly?" I asked.

"This is a good settlement, Kate. A really good settlement."

"Walk me through the payout terms. I'm not sure I can think straight."

"For the first year you'll receive a payment equal to the greater of two million dollars or the amount due under the terms of the riders. At the end of that year, Encore can purchase all of your remaining rights under your existing contract for an amount equal to two times that amount."

"And what is this about the June 1st payment?"

"You'll receive a one million dollar advance on June first."

"That's less than two weeks away!"

"I know!" Glenn said, with an excitement that came from being my friend more so than my lawyer.

"I agree with Glenn," Eliot said in a more moderate tone. "It's an excellent offer. However, if this show turns out to be extremely successful, you might be leaving a lot of money on the table."

"I'm looking at six million dollars here, maybe even more. I thought I was only entitled to seventy five thousand. I'll take it. I don't want to be greedy, and I think if we push them too much they'll either drop the show or tie me up in court. Do you agree, Glenn?"

"As your lawyer, I think it's reasonable to accept the offer. As your friend, I don't want to see you risk any portion of this windfall."

Eliot, who had the clearest head of the three of us, pointed out that the new settlement contract obligated me to participate in a reunion show, appear on a few promotional talk shows and maintain a blog on their website.

"That's fine, Eliot. I don't mind. I don't have any real job prospects at this point anyway. I have the time. Let's sign this sucker before they change their minds!"

The three of us put on our poker faces and walked back into the conference room. The Encore suits looked relieved when we accepted their offer. I signed the settlement contract, Encore's representatives signed, Helen notarized our signatures, and it was done. The woman from the Encore team shook my hand and welcomed me to the Encore family.

Elaine looked like she was going to throw up.

Chapter 14

The day the bank called to tell me the one million dollar wire from Encore had hit my account, I broke down and cried. All the worry and tension I'd experienced during the past eight months came pouring out.

After an hour, I was all cried out and left with a strange sense of peace along with a dull headache. I took two Advil and then a hot shower. I stood under the punishing stream of water until my fingers puckered and my skin was almost raw. I dried off with the plush white towels Angela had given me as a shower gift. The towels, while still soft, had begun to unravel at the edges, much like the marriage they were meant to celebrate.

I looked at myself in the mirror and could see that, thanks to my daily walks with Lucy, I had lost a few pounds and my legs appeared slimmer and more toned. Even my ass, the bane of my existence since I was twelve, appeared firmer. No one would confuse me with a Playboy centerfold, but for forty two, I didn't look too bad.

I wrapped myself in a soft terrycloth robe and called Paul.

"Kate, I'm glad you called. I've been thinking of you. What are you doing?"

"I just got out of the shower."

"Are you still naked?"

I laughed. "I have a robe on, you perv. Listen, it's not that kind of call. I received my first settlement payment this morning, and I have the urge to celebrate. Can you make it back to Centre Island tonight?"

"Absolutely."

"Good. Listen, why don't I arrange dinner at your house? I'd like you all to myself tonight."

"Sounds good to me," Paul said. "The key is under the flowerpot next to the garage. I can get there by seven."

"Perfect. I'll have everything ready."

"I can't wait, babe."

My parents were thrilled and relieved by news of my settlement--I think we were all unable to believe it until the money actually came in. My mother had finished *On the Shores of the Shannon* and was happy to watch Lucy. I picked Lucy up from nursery school and dropped her off at my parents' house. I then ordered a sumptuous meal from Cora's Concepts in Catering and picked up two bottles of champagne.

I got to Paul's at six, wearing a soft cotton sundress over a low cut lacy bra and matching panties--no rubber undergarments this time. My skin glistened with moisturizer, and I wore a light, subtle scent--nothing to clash with the stronger spicy cologne I suspected Paul would pour on tonight. At some point I was going to have to break him of that habit. The catering people, right on time, set up the meal on sternos. I rummaged through Paul's china cabinet until I came up with a set of plates, crystal wine goblets and a pair of silver candlestick holders. I set the small table on his deck overlooking the Sound rather than his formal dining room--I didn't want him to think of Thanksgiving dinners with his ex while I was trying to seduce him. I was lighting the candles when I felt two arms circle my waist.

"You're early," I scolded.

"I know. Forgive me, I couldn't wait," Paul said, turning me to face him. He reached down and kissed me hard. I pressed against him. A whoop of approval boomed from the two young fisherman in a cabin cruiser anchored about forty feet off Paul's dock.

"We'd better take this inside unless you want to give those guys a show," he said. With not a thought for the chicken francese bubbling away on its sterno, I followed Paul to his bedroom. I suspected that he'd refurnished this room after his divorce because it was a medley of masculine dark greens and reds, a relief since I didn't want my first post-Jim sexual experience to take place in another woman's floral sheets.

Paul relieved me of my dress and lacy bra, driving all thoughts of floral bedding from my mind. He pushed me down on the bed and tore off his tie and striped collared shirt. His chest was more muscular than I would have thought, and his left arm had a jagged scar I found oddly attractive. While Paul certainly didn't have Jim's dark handsome looks, he was rugged and manly in a way that right now I found even more compelling.

Paul gave me one of his crooked smiles and then lay down beside me, cupping my breasts. I said not a word as his lips explored my body. Just when I thought I couldn't stand it anymore, Paul moved against me as we came together.

I dozed, satisfied and content.

Paul stroked my hair. "Babe," he whispered, "did you leave something on the stove?"

I shot up and ran naked to the kitchen, probably giving my fisherman friends quite a thrill as I lifted the foil cover of the chicken francese. Much of the sauce had evaporated, but the chicken hadn't burned. I blew out the sterno and returned to the bedroom, diving under the covers. My sprint to the kitchen must have given Paul some ideas because round two soon commenced.

Instead of craving sleep afterward, we both craved food, so wearing one of Paul's robes--he refused to allow me to get dressed--I heated up the chicken and the additional sauce Cora's had supplied. Paul poured the champagne, and we began to devour the chicken and pasta. As Paul remarked about how refreshing it was to be with a woman who enjoyed food, we heard a car drive up the gravel driveway. Paul looked surprised, and my stomach dropped at the thought of the angry ex-wife interrupting our little love nest. He left the table to answer the door while I ran into his bedroom to get dressed. I didn't look too bad, aside from my flushed cheeks and unruly hair.

As I entered the living room I saw several suitcases and garment bags. I walked onto the deck to find Don, pale and drawn, holding a glass of whisky.

He looked up at me and didn't seem to notice anything strange about my appearance. He just stared and said, "She's kicked me out. That bitch has thrown me out of my own house."

"Have you eaten, Don? We have plenty of food, let me make you a plate," I said.

He didn't respond. I loaded the remains of our romantic meal onto a plain white plate, walked back out to the deck and landed the plate in front of him. Like a robot, Don ate the chicken. No one said anything. We just listened to the whir of the boats passing by. I stood to make coffee and serve dessert. Paul followed me into the kitchen where he kissed me.

"Kate, I'm sorry he's ruined our evening. Still, I can't throw him out after what he's been through."

"It's fine. Although I expect you to make it up to me."

Paul carried in the coffee pot while I cut each of us a generous slice of cheesecake. The dinner had seemed to lift Don's spirits and at last he was able to speak.

"The timing couldn't be worse," Don said. "My lawyers have just inked a deal with the SEC. *The Journal* is running an article tomorrow."

"So where did you come out with the SEC?" Paul asked.

"My attorneys and investigators were able to determine that John Glick and Tom Harris were the guilty traders. But it's my company, I'm ultimately responsible, so I'll be paying a huge fine to the SEC and I'm shutting down my funds. The SEC is also imposing a one year suspension of my securities licenses. All in all, it's not a bad deal, and I won't do any jail time. How about you, Paul?"

"All the SEC came up with was some bullshit technical violation based on the fact the sales materials I used were inaccurate because they reflected Glick's and Harris's improper trades. Like I could have known that. I didn't want this thing to drag on, though. I agreed to pay the fine without any admission of wrongdoing. It was only fifty grand, so no big deal."

I smiled at Paul. We'd been so busy satisfying out animal urges that we hadn't had a chance to catch up on his SEC problems. I was relieved things had worked out so well for him. I then looked at Don, whose jaw was set in anger.

"Don, all things considered, I think you did quite well," I said using my lawyer voice. "In this environment, the government usually wants to use the big guys as scapegoats. I think it says a lot for your integrity and standing in the hedge fund community that the sanctions weren't more severe. With such a good result, why did Pamela throw you out?"

"I've embarrassed her. And she says I'm impacting her career. 'What career?' I asked her, and then she threw a vase at me. I mean, come on--she hasn't worked since she got pregnant with Diana. And before that, well, you know," he said, looking at me.

Paul looked somewhat confused. I guess he wasn't aware of Pamela's and Don's alternative lifestyle, which was a relief to me. Part of me was afraid I'd find out Paul kept whips and chains in the back of his truck.

Don took a swig of wine. "I've subsidized those ridiculous charities and that stupid entertaining book. I even agreed to appear on that idiotic show. Now for the first time I'm asking something of her, to support me and stand by me, and she kicks me to the curb. I'll tell you Paul, Suzanne would've never pulled something like this."

Paul nodded.

Don continued, "Well, she's out of her mind if she thinks she's taking my daughter and getting any money out of me. Our pre-nup is iron-clad, and if she thinks I'll just roll over because I don't want any more bad press, she's got another thing coming. Even after the fine, I'll never need to work again. I don't really give a damn what anyone says about me."

Don poured himself another tumbler of whisky and then looked at me. The lights must have finally gone on because he turned red. "I'm such an idiot. I'm interrupting something here, aren't I?"

"Don, it's quite all right. I need to get going anyway."

"Kate, Paul, I'm sorry," Don said, "I can find a hotel."

"Don't be silly," I said. "I need to pick up my daughter anyway."

"Let me walk you out," Paul said.

I tried not to feel resentful of the fact that once again Pamela Kruger had interrupted our time together, but Paul's warm kiss goodnight melted some of that resentment away.

Chapter 15

Encore's first *Gold Coast Wives* episode aired in early June, days after I'd received my million dollar payment. Unlike Channel 45's six episode season, Encore's season would consist of nine episodes. I wondered what lost footage of mine would surface--they couldn't possibly find any more embarrassing ass shots. Encore had pulled out all the stops promoting what they hoped would be their summer reality hit. We'd made the covers of three magazines as well.

My slim hope that my former colleagues would somehow miss the *Gold Coast Wives* hoopla was dashed when I saw Glenn Meyers and Eliot Hansen on the June fifth cover of the *Manhattan Law Journal*. The *MLJ* pitted Meyers and Finkel as the winners of a David and Goliath-type fight with the network. A picture of me taken two years ago wearing a dark suit and pearls was splashed in the corner next to a shot of me dancing with Paul in my blood-red finale gown. By June 6th my in-box was flooded with emails from former clients and colleagues. Some of the younger Fowler Sherman associates had posted to my Encore blog. Most of the emails were positive and congratulatory since the *MLJ* piece focused on the legal arguments employed by Meyers and Finkel and the arbitrator's respect for the integrity of my contract. Of course the fact I received such a high settlement impressed people. Would they be as impressed when they saw me stuffing my mouth with donuts and calling people bitches? The jury was still out on that one.

I responded to most of the emails with short notes of thanks. For closer friends, such as Shari Gruber, I wrote somewhat longer notes of explanation and told them I would be in touch as soon as everything died down. I even heard from Kyle Madden, who apparently was a huge fan of the show. Kyle was surprised when I told him I still wanted to continue my job search. He was unsure whether the show would help or harm my prospects.

I hadn't seen Paul since our dinner at his place because he'd been tied up finalizing his deal with the SEC, and of course his houseguest didn't help matters. Paul suggested we meet at my house. I shot that one right down. Lucy was confused enough about her father leaving, I was not about to compound the problem by introducing another man into the mix. Not at this point anyway. For the moment, we had to make do with sexy phone talk until Don found other living arrangements.

My father had finally bought a gas grill, so on a sunny Saturday afternoon in late June he invited us over to sample some charred meat. Lucy was excited because she loved swimming in my parent's ancient above-ground pool. I was excited because I didn't have to spend yet another afternoon at the Fleets Cove Beach and Tennis Club trying not to notice the whispers and stares. I loaded Lucy, her swimming paraphernalia and the German potato salad I'd made myself and headed south to my parents' house in Massapequa. I found Deirdre and my mother huddled around my mother's laptop while Gordon and my father worked the grill and made sure that Lindsay and Brendan didn't drown.

Deirdre looked up from the screen. "Could your blog commentary this week be any more boring?"

"Oh, please, you're not really reading that thing are you?" I asked as I searched for room in my mother's overcrowded fridge for my potato salad.

"Of course we're reading it. You should read some of the comments based on yesterday's episode," my sister said.

"Oh, I missed yesterday's episode. Did they show anything new?" I asked as I pulled off Lucy's t-shirt and helped her into her bathing suit.

"I think there were a few more close-ups of your hives but nothing else new," my mother said.

"No, the interesting thing is what HellCat1 wrote in the commentary section of your blog. She, well I'm assuming HellCat1 is a she, said she received Pamela's gray tablecloth as a wedding gift four years ago, along with the matching napkins, so there is no way that it's a family heirloom. She said Pamela is a liar."

"Oh, I knew Pamela lied about that. What's the big deal?"

"Apparently, your blog friends think it's a big deal, and your fans are stirring it up over on Pamela's page," Deirdre said.

"Fans? I don't think I have any fans."

"You do now," Deirdre said.

"Great. Deranged fans, that's all I need. Please, turn the damn thing off."

"What did they say about me again?" my mother asked, scrolling down my blog like an IT expert.

"Oh, RealityLove said you were 'feisty and fun' and that *The Lady and the Rogue* is one of her favorite books."

"See, they're not all deranged."

"Off, off now!" I reached for the laptop.

"Now that you're a millionaire, you're no fun."

"And your blog is terrible, Kate. It's like you're just dialing it in," my mother scolded.

"Mom, I *am* just dialing it in. My settlement contract said I had to write a three hundred word post after every aired episode, and that's what I write."

"It's not fair to the viewers. Pamela's was at least three pages this week."

"And Tina responds to bloggers' questions."

"Questions?" I scoffed. "What kind of questions are viewers asking Tina? What her cup size is?"

"Among other things," Deirdre said.

"Fine, hand me that thing." I clicked onto my blog. "Okay, how does this sound? 'Dear Viewers, I'm sitting here at my mother's kitchen table doing, what else, drinking tea and eating donuts.'"

"But you're not eating donuts, Kate," my mother said.

"People now think I eat donuts all the time. I might as well go with it. Anyway, let's continue. 'My mother and Dee are complaining about my blog. They say I'm just dialing it in, and, dear viewers, I fear that they may be right. In order to spice things up, I will answer three viewers' questions every week. The questions can be on any topic you like. Thanks for your support and kind comments, and I look forward to receiving your questions.' There, how was that?"

"It's a start anyway," said Deirdre.

"Girls," my father said, sticking his head in the door, "it's a beautiful day outside. Get out here and have some meat!"

We loaded up the condiments, salads, cups, plates, forks and knives and joined my father, Gordon and the kids. I know it's un-American, but I'm not a big fan of the barbecue. I feel like I'm always making a million trips in and out and by the time I sit down my food is cold, and I hate it when my food gets cold. Anyway, we all praised my father's burgers, even though they were a little on the well done side. But hey, he was trying, and the kids liked them, even my finicky lady.

As I was packing up to leave, my mother clicked onto the Encore website. "Kate, you already have twenty five questions!"

"How many are about my bra size?" I asked as I dragged a comb through Lucy's snarled curls.

"Five. There are some other good ones here. Like, 'Who is the most influential person in your life?'"

"Oh, God, I hate questions like that. It's like when I was interviewing for jobs in law school and someone asked me if I was an animal what kind would I be?"

"What did you say?" Deirdre asked.

"A little fluffy bunny. No, of course I didn't say that. I think I said tiger or lion or something terribly aggressive like that. Questions like that are usually pointless because no one ever tells the truth. I'd rather tell people my bra size."

"Tell them your bra size," Deirdre said. "I dare you."

I grabbed the computer and typed in the following:

Here are the answers to the first three questions received:

1. I am a 38D--eat your hearts out, all you skinny bitches out there.

2. Yes, I know sugar is bad for children's teeth, but sometimes I don't care.

3. See answer to question 1 above.

Chapter 16

The next five weeks flew by. Lucy seemed to shoot up all of a sudden, and somehow my little baby had turned into a smart, sassy little girl. I filled our summer days with trips to the beach, swimming lessons, picnics with my new yummy mummy friends and backyard barbecues with various members of the extended Griffin clan.

Gold Coast Wives attracted an increasing audience, and Encore considered the show a surprise summer hit. The promotion budget was fairly large for a cable reality show, and Encore had blanketed Manhattan with posters of the four Wives. One day Shari had called me excitedly to report that she had taken a crosstown bus that morning with my big ole face plastered on the side of it. So much for staying under the radar.

I stayed fairly close to home most of the summer and insulated myself as much as possible from the *Gold Coast Wives* static. Unlike my fellow Wives, I kept my public appearances to the minimum required under my settlement agreement. I did have fun answering viewers' questions on the blog, but unlike my sister who had developed an unhealthy obsession with all things Wives, I kept my surfing to a minimum.

I couldn't resist watching the new episodes. Unlike the previous iteration, the latest presentation of my life was much more balanced, and I was shown as more than just a donut-obsessed mess. Initially I had been upset Encore had included certain conversations in my kitchen I considered private and didn't know were caught on camera, such as my conversations with my mother about Jim. However, the overall reaction from viewers was positive, and I believe it created a certain amount of sympathy for me. In fact, Deirdre said there was a *We Love Kate* site comprised primarily of divorced mothers.

Rachel's and Pamela's portrayals, however, were much more negative than they'd been during Channel 45's season. Encore had included several scenes in which Rachel berated poor Garrett until he cried. The cameras had even caught one scene where Rachel screamed at a waitress who brought her the wrong bottle of wine. Pamela's scenes with Don were almost painful to watch at times. He appeared disconnected from her, often unable to restrain himself from rolling his eyes whenever she discussed one of her *passions*. And of course, unlike Channel 45's version, Encore devoted almost an entire episode to the dinner scene from Wolf Lodge Casino, with several close ups of Pamela in her dominatrix paraphernalia. One of the cameras caught Angela calling her a prostitute. Even I began to thaw and feel a bit sorry for her.

Speaking of Don, he'd finally moved out of Paul's house. Paul had had a heavy summer traveling schedule, meeting with several big clients in London and Berlin. Although we'd only spent a few nights together, each had been as delicious as our first encounter. Our dates consisted of dinner, wine, flowers, and decadent non-marital sex. It was as if I were on a Spring Break for the heart.

I entered the Encore soundstage on a muggy July afternoon with a clear head, a slight summer tan and a healthy bank account. I felt so unlike the sad shell of a woman who had stood on Pamela's doorstep months earlier. Wearing a white linen pants suit accompanied by a pair of silver owl earrings, I felt young and carefree. After the afternoon's taping of the reunion show, I would be released from all remaining obligations to Encore at last. While I was still ambivalent about my strange new fame, the financial stability it had provided was a great comfort.

I arrived early to be styled by Jenna, the young woman who'd replaced Chris. Encore had hired Chris to host a new makeover show called *I Can't Believe You're Wearing That*, and while I missed him, Jenna was certainly much less bossy and critical. After Jenna had arranged my hair into a soft, relaxed updo in a way that camouflaged my sticky-outy ears, she slathered a thick layer of base makeup on my face which she swore couldn't possibly irritate my skin. Another young girl, an assistant something or other, showed me to a small waiting room stacked with magazines, Evian and Snickers bars. The assistant to the assistant nervously told me that I wouldn't see the other Wives until the cameras were rolling. She looked surprised when I gave her a smile--I think she half expected me to call her a bitch or throw a donut at her or something.

I had made it through two trashy mags by the time the little assistant came back to fetch me. The girl led me through a long corridor that opened up into a large industrial space. At the center on a raised platform was a faux living room. On the back wall hung a large sign with the now familiar *Gold Coast Wives* logo in fancy gold script. Two long brown leather couches faced each other with a large armchair separating them. The blinding lights bleached out everything, which explained why Jenna had been so heavy-handed with the makeup. Tina, looking every inch the star in tight black pants and four inch heels, sat on one of the couches. The assistant directed me to sit next to her.

We had just kissed hello when Pamela and Rachel joined us and sat on the opposite couch. Pamela looked elegant in a soft lavender cocktail dress. Rachel looked a bit drawn in an apricot summer suit that didn't suit her olive skin. Rachel and Pamela both gave Tina an enthusiastic hello while I received curt nods, making me wonder if they had rehearsed their greetings at home. As Pamela busied herself smoothing the skirt of her dress, a tall, thin man with highlighted blond hair strode onto the set. He gave us a wide smile that exposed his rather large, overly white teeth.

"Ladies, welcome. I'm Spence Greenley, your host for the evening. I'm glad you could all make it," he said, as if we had a choice.

"Now, relax and try to enjoy yourselves," he said to Rachel who was looking a bit green. "We're going to discuss what you've been up to since taping ended and take some questions from viewers. This will be shown live, but don't let that throw you. Okay?" he asked as we all nodded.

The new theme song Encore had developed for the show boomed from the speakers. Rachel jumped at the sound. The lights became even brighter, and I noticed there were more than five cameras. When the music died down, our man Spence looked at the center camera like a pro and said, "Welcome to the *Gold Coast Wives* reunion show, where we'll catch up with our favorite Long Island wives, live, as they fill us in on everything that's happened since the explosive finale!" The music keyed up again as I supposed they cut for a commercial break. We looked at each other, somewhat confused as to what we were supposed to do now, when the music blared again.

Spence looked at the camera and smiled. "Tina Andrews, beloved long time star of *Hope's Glen*, brought her special blend of sexiness and spirituality to this season of *Gold Coast Wives*. Let's take a look." And with that the show's sign transformed itself into a large screen, where we were treated to a montage of Tina doing yoga in her microscopic leotard, sailing with one of her boy toys and practicing her lines with Rachel, of all people. "Tina, tell us what you've been up to since the finale."

"Oh, Spence," Tina said in her breathy voice, "I've just been so busy developing my new line of yoga clothing. It's called *Gold Coast Moves by Tina Andrews* and is available at most department stores and at TinaAndrews.com."

"Sounds fascinating, Tina."

"I've also started taping for *Hope's Glen*. I return to the show next month, and there are many surprises in store for Camilla Yardley."

"Oh, Tina, I'm so happy for you," I blurted out. I hated the idea of Tina being shunted aside because she was on the wrong side of forty.

Spence and Tina both looked surprised by my outburst.

Tina grabbed my hand and smiled. "Thanks, Kate. I know how much you enjoy the show. If you'd like, I could get you a back stage pass."

"Oh, Tina, I would love that. Thank you."

Rachel looked put out at being excluded, so she interjected, "I've also been busy this summer, Spence."

"Yes, Rachel. How was your summer? You must have been exhausted after all your work on the LICKs Ball." Somewhere my sister was giggling.

"Oh, I was. And despite the distractions certain people caused," she said glaring at me, "it was a wonderful success, and we raised a ton of money for kitty rescue."

"You did an amazing job, Rachel," chimed in her sidekick Pamela.

"Thank you, sweetie. I couldn't have done it without your help." I suspected Pamela did not so much as stuff an envelope, but I let it pass.

"And once you recovered from all your efforts," Spence said without a trace of irony, "what then?"

"Oh, Finley's Fine Furnishings, the premier design center on the North Shore, has kept me very busy. We just launched our new line, Gold Coast Living, now available at our Huntington location and online. It was inspired by the project we did for the, uh, Ryans." Rachel didn't even look in my direction.

"Let's take a look, Rachel," Spence said, as a montage of Rachel's season highlights was shown on the giant screen. Rachel was shown bossing Garrett and fussing over the crystal cats in my great room, screaming at another underling at Finley's, hugging her two sons and winning at craps at Wolf Lodge casino. Of course the montage ended with her screaming at me and ordering me out of the LICKs Ball. Not knowing what expression to wear, I simply tried to look blank, as if sitting in a particularly boring tax conference.

"Rachel, have you and Kate spoken since the show finished taping?"

"No," Rachel snapped.

"I've spoken to her husband," I said, "who apologized for her hurtful remarks and behavior at the finale."

"*My* behavior? Why would David need to apologize for my behavior?" Rachel screeched.

"Do you really want to get into that with me, Rachel?" I asked, raising my eyebrows.

Visions of brawny Irishman with bagpipes picketing her store must have been dancing in Rachel's head when she croaked, "Let's forget it. Move on, Spence."

While Spence looked confused by Rachel's sudden retreat, he moved onto Pamela like a pro. The Krugers' divorce and Don's SEC investigation had received a lot of local press, as did Pamela's past as a leather queen, so I was curious to see what type of softball Spence was going to lob at her.

"Pamela," Spence said as he took her hand, "your family's been in the papers in the last few weeks. Would you care to comment?"

"It's been a difficult time, Spence. A very difficult time. But I have good friends," she said, smiling at Rachel, "who have helped me get through it. And work. I've traveled the country promoting my book, *Gold Coast Entertaining*, where I've had the opportunity to share my love of entertaining with so many people. My charity work has also provided so much solace. Helping others sometimes has the added benefit of helping yourself."

"True. So true, Pamela," Rachel said.

"I've also been busy putting the finishing touches on my second book, *Gold Coast Entertaining At Night*." The new cover flashed on the screen.

Oh, my God. The woman had no shame. Pamela, draped along a high wooden dining room table, was wearing a black leather bustier and thigh high boots and carrying a teeny tiny whip. "Nice cover," I said.

She gave me a triumphant smile. "Oh, I knew you'd love it, Kate."

"With all this going on, Pamela, how have you been coping?" Rachel asked.

"Of course, to find out your husband is a criminal, well you can just imagine." Pamela managed to squeeze out a few tears.

"You poor thing," Rachel cooed.

"Wait a second," I said. "Don's not a criminal."

"He's an inside trader, Kate," Pamela snapped.

"No, he's not. Some of his employees were engaged in insider trading. There's no evidence that Don was involved. He may be guilty of not supervising his employees properly, and he has been sanctioned by the SEC, but to say he's a criminal, well, that's not accurate."

"Kate, as far as I'm concerned, he's a criminal," Pamela said.

"Believe it or not Pamela, just because *you* say something, doesn't make it true. Don's paid a fine, that doesn't make him a criminal. And for you to call him one on live TV is wrong. You can call me a whore and tell people I was a slut in high school, but again, just because you say it doesn't make it true."

"You seem very concerned about my husband, Kate. Maybe you should focus a little more on your own. Where is he this week, trekking through Antarctica?" Pamela said with a smirk. Rachel gave her a high five.

"We're separated. I've filed a petition for divorce based on abandonment," I said with as much dignity as I could muster.

"Given the way you threw yourself at my brother-in-law, I'm not surprised he's abandoned you." A picture of Paul and me dancing at the finale flashed on the screen.

"You know what, Pamela, I don't care what you think. True, when I met Paul I was still married. However, at that point my husband had been gone for months. I didn't start dating Paul until after I filed for divorce."

"If you don't care what I think, then why are you commenting on my marriage? Why are you and your pathetic sister so concerned about my past? Digging around like little Nancy Drews. So sad."

"I'm not commenting on your marriage, I'm just defending the reputation of an icon in the hedge fund community and a man I believe to be maligned by you."

"Why don't you admit that you're obsessed with me? Come on, everyone saw it on the show. You were always talking about me, you even commented on my boobs for heaven's sake."

"Pamela, you're right. I allowed you to rattle me in high school, and I allowed you to rattle me on the show. But that stops now." I was so upset, I started to hyperventilate.

"Are you okay, Kate? Why don't we take a break. We'll be right back with more revelations from the fascinating Gold Coast Wives," Spence said as the music came on.

My breathing slowed down. I took a drink of water from the glass an assistant handed me and looked at my watch. Another hour of this torture and then I never had to look that bitch in the face again.

The *Gold Coast Wives* theme blasted through the speakers again, and we were off.

"Kate, what have you been up to since the finale?" Spence asked, as if the dust up between me and Pamela a few moments ago had never happened.

"Nothing much, Spence. I've just been home spending time with my daughter and my family. I've also started dating Paul."

"No books, no other projects?"

"I'm still looking for a legal job, but no. No other projects," I said.

"Why should she work? She's too busy taking a piece of our action," Rachel said.

"What do you mean, Rachel?" Spence asked, looking confused.

"I said," Rachel enunciated in a louder voice, "why should she work when she's getting a percentage of all our projects. I heard from the station last week that if I want to call my new furniture collection the Gold Coast Collection I have to pay Encore a percentage, most of which will be paid to Kate."

"Is that true?" Tina said, turning to me.

"Yes, if the producers haven't called you yet, they will. All products that use the name Gold Coast will have to pay a percentage to Kate," Rachel said.

"So I have to pay you for my yoga clothes?" Tina asked, her voice hard and very unlike Marilyn's.

"Please don't tell me I have to pay her anything from my books." Pamela looked at Rachel.

"Call your lawyer when we're done. I think that's how it works," Rachel said.

"But why?" Tina asked.

"Before I signed the contract, I sent it to be reviewed by an expert in entertainment law. He negotiated a good contract for me."

"That's not fair!" Tina said, almost shouting. It looked like I wouldn't be getting those back stage passes after all.

"Listen, it's not my fault you didn't negotiate a better deal," I said, trying not to raise my voice.

"Is it true you got paid a million dollars?" Rachel asked.

"A million dollars!" Tina screeched.

"I'm not discussing the terms of my contract with you."

The other women looked at me with impotent fury but couldn't think of anything to say in response. There was silence for a few moments while the women continued to glower at me, even my former semi-friend Tina.

Spence finally broke the silence by saying, "Kate, you have certainly been one of the more controversial Wives this season. Let's take a look."

I watched the screen and saw myself tossing a ball to Lucy on my front lawn. There were several shots of me eating cake and donuts at my kitchen table. I'd pretty much expected some of that. No shock there. The screen flashed the finale scenes with Rachel yelling at me, and Paul and I circling the dance floor. Again, I'd expected this to be shown. They closed with a scene that hadn't been part of the show, something which I hadn't realized had been filmed. It was the conversation Deirdre and I'd had in my kitchen about Jim and how I'd always been afraid he'd leave me. Against my will, my eyes filled with tears. This was something I could barely say to myself, never mind to millions of strangers.

Someone must have handed me a tissue because I was really crying now. I felt a man's hand on my shoulder, and I assumed Spence had walked over to comfort me. When I looked up, it wasn't Spence. It was Jim.

"Sweetheart, don't cry. Please don't cry."

"Jim?"

He gathered me in his arms and stroked my hair. For a moment, it was as if everyone in the studio had melted away and it was only me and Jim, in each other's arms. For a moment I was overwhelmed with relief that he was home.

And then that moment passed.

I pushed him away. "What the hell are you doing here?"

"I wanted to surprise you," he said, looking even more gorgeous than I'd remembered. Jim had always been handsome, but now that handsomeness was tougher somehow, more rugged. He was dressed in jeans and a t-shirt, arms rippled with muscles that hadn't been there a year ago.

"Well," I said, "you succeeded. Now leave."

"I knew you wouldn't see me, so I called Deirdre and she told me about the taping. I figured if I just showed up here, you'd have to speak to me."

"I've been trying to speak to you for months and you pick now? In front of millions of strangers? Now you want to talk?"

"My mother sent me tapes of the show. Until I saw them, I guess I hadn't realized how much I'd hurt you. I was caught up in my own disappointment. I didn't think about what I was doing to you and Lucy. I thought you were capable, that you could handle anything," Jim said.

"Well, you can see how I've handled things. All our dirty laundry hanging out for the world to see."

Jim touched my cheek. "You know what I saw on those tapes, Kate? I saw a beautiful, funny, loving woman, fighting for her family. I saw a woman who never gave up. I saw the woman I fell in love with so many years ago. The woman I was a fool to leave." Jim's eyes glistened with tears.

"Why Jim? Why did you leave?"

"Kate, I felt like such a failure. I thought you didn't really need me. And then, traveling around with a bunch of young guys, living out in that wild country, I was another person. I was free, free in a way I don't think I've ever felt. No responsibilities, no deadlines. I guess I got caught up in it. But when you said you wanted a divorce, and then when I saw the tapes, I realized how stupid and selfish I'd been. Can you forgive me, Kate?"

"I don't know, Jim." I sobbed as he swept me up in his arms.

Chapter 17

How I got through the remainder of the taping I'll never know. The nervous teenage assistant took Jim to the green room while another assistant led me back to my seat.

The *Gold Coast Wives* theme music blared, the hot studio lights blasted and we were off again.

"You certainly know how to bring the drama, Kate, don't you?" Spence asked.

"What?"

"Oh, you don't need to act so innocent, Kate," Pamela snarked. "You really didn't know your husband was back in town?"

"No! Of course not."

"Well, I for one don't believe her. Anything to bring the spotlight back on 'poor little Kate.' I'm sick of it," Rachel whined. "We're all sick of it."

My head pounded with the start of a migraine. "I didn't know. I don't know what else to tell you."

All fake sympathy, Spence took my hand. "Kate, we only have a few minutes left, but can you share with the audience how you're feeling? Are you happy that Jim is back? What about Paul?"

"Yeah, Kate," Pamela said, her eyes glistening with malice, "what about poor Paul?"

The clip of me and Paul dancing at the LICKs Ball played on the screen behind Spence's head.

Oh my God, Paul. I hadn't even thought about Paul.

The four of them stared at me. I had to say something. But what?

I took a deep breath and looked in the camera and pretended I was speaking directly to Deirdre and not to millions of viewers. "When Jim left for Australia, I didn't allow myself to think about him leaving me. Not really. For the first few weeks I used to pretend he was working late. Because, it might be hard for you understand this, but Jim was my life.

He is the only man I've ever loved. Hell, maybe he's the only man I'll ever love.

"But you can only lie to yourself for so long, and as weeks turned into months I had to admit that he was gone. There were nights when the house was quiet, when Lucy was in bed, that I thought I would die. I really did. But my daughter, my family, this ridiculous show were my lifeline. They kept me busy, and while I was worrying about paying the mortgage and whether all of America thought I was a fat pig, I didn't have time to face the fact that the love of my life was gone. That he had left me and didn't love me anymore.

"I know I should have thought about what I would do if Jim ever came back. But I didn't. I couldn't allow myself to hope that he'd come back."

"But now he has," Tina said, her beautiful arctic eyes full of sympathy.

"Yes. Now he has. And I don't know what I'm going to do. That's the truth."

"Do you love him, Kate? Do you?" Tina asked.

Tears filled my eyes. "God help me, Tina, but I think I do."

* * * *

The white linen suit that had looked so clean, so crisp a few short hours ago hung on me, damp with sweat and wrinkled like a used tissue. Tendrils of hair had escaped the tasteful twist and were now pasted to my forehead, trapped by the heavy makeup and perspiration. But no matter how horrible I looked, it couldn't compare to how horrible I felt.

The air was refrigerator cool in the green room and Jim…well, Jim looked like he had stepped off the cover of one of my mother's Heartland romances, all rippled muscles and smoky eyes. I didn't have the energy to be self-conscious as I collapsed onto the hard leather couch opposite him.

"So," I said to my errant husband.

He smiled his heartbreaking smile. "So."

"What now?"

He rose from the couch and took my face in his hands and kissed me. The kiss that I had imagined for so long, Jim's homecoming kiss, was sweet and it was sad. And it left me feeling somewhat empty.

"You haven't answered my question, Jim."

"We go home, sweetheart. We go home."

Despite myself, I laughed. "A kiss and a hug and I'm supposed to pretend that the last nine months never happened? Sorry, Jim, but you'll have to do better than that."

He took my hand. "Tell me what you want, Kate. Tell me what you want me to do, and I'll do it."

A wave of exhaustion swept over me. "You know what? I'm tired of being the adult. Tired of making all the decisions, tired of carrying the bag. Why don't you tell me what you want for our family?"

"I want this to go back to how things were."

"The way things were? But Jim, you ran away from the way things were. It can't just have been the job, there must have been some other reason why you left me, left your child."

"I was an idiot, Katie. I admitted that to you already. I was fool to leave you."

"Yes, Jim, you were. But if we're going to do this, then we're going to do this right. Take it slow. Become reacquainted with each other. I've changed, Jim. I've changed so much these past few months."

He touched my cheek. "You haven't changed to me. You're still that girl I fell for in the Hamptons."

"No, Jim. You're not listening. I *have* changed. Listen, I'm too tired to do this now. Why don't you call me in a couple of days and we'll decide what to do then."

"A couple of days?" Jim kissed me again, not gentle like before but urgent, forceful. He whispered into my ear. "Do you really want to wait?"

I could never resist Jim. I could never resist his kisses and his deep sexy voice. Almost as if watching myself on a TV screen, I heard myself say, "Yes, Jim. I really do want to wait a few days. You have my cell, give me a call next week." And with that I picked up the Birkin bag I had treated myself to, and for the first time since that fateful night in the Hamptons, I walked away from Jim.

* * * *

Dr. Frank's office was a man cave personified: dark wood paneling, brown leather chairs, plaid couch. The only feminine touch was the large box of tissues in the center of the coffee table, tissues I'd managed to avoid using in our previous three sessions.

Dr. Frank smiled at me as we waited for Jim to arrive. Jim was late for couples counseling. Again.

The grandfather clock ticked in the background as Dr. Frank and I chatted about the recent heat wave.

Ten minutes later Jim barreled into the office, dressed in his favorite fishing shirt and rumpled khaki shorts, smelling of suntan lotion and sweat.

"Sorry, I'm late, Katie, Dr. Frank. We had some trouble with the boat." He smiled at me, his typical naughty little boy smile.

"You went fishing? I thought you were having lunch in the city with your old boss?" I asked, hating myself for sounding like such a scold.

"Oh well, ah, he cancelled."

"Bob cancelled?" I snapped. "Jesus, Jim, had you even scheduled a lunch with him, or was that something you said to get me off your back?"

"Relax, hon. I'll call him next week to reschedule."

"I believe, Jim, that this was the third work-related lunch that's been cancelled," Dr. Frank said in his professional, non-accusatory voice. "Perhaps we should talk about your feelings about finding work."

Jim was sprawled across the plain couch. "It's pointless. The economy sucks."

"It's not pointless," I said. "Things are picking up. I even got a call about a general counsel position last week. My first interview is on Tuesday."

"Well, little miss perfect got an interview. Good for you," Jim snarled.

I felt like I'd been slapped. I fought back the sting of tears, and said in a calm voice, "Yes, good for me. Good for us. So that we can both get back to work and get back on track."

"Jim, what are your plans?" Dr. Frank asked.

"Aside from fishing and drinking beer," I added. Dr. Frank gave me a look. "Sorry. That was unnecessary. Go on, Jim, tell me what you want to do."

"I don't know yet. I want to relax, get back together with friends. Move home and live with my wife and daughter."

"Jim, we talked about that. I don't think that's such a good idea. Not until I'm sure that this is going to work."

"Damn it, Kate, I don't know why you're riding me so much. Who cares if I get a job? You have plenty of money."

"Yes, I did receive a small settlement, but I'm using that for Lucy's college fund and to pay off the mortgage."

"Small settlement? Is that right, Kate? I wouldn't call six million dollars small."

I looked at him for a moment, sprawled out on that couch like an overgrown frat boy. So defiant, so smug. After a few moments, I said, "Wait a minute, how do you know how big my settlement was? I never told you, and the amount never made the papers."

"My mother told me."

"Okay, my Dad must have told Sean." I felt my stomach drop. "When did you find out, Jim?"

"I've known for a while," Jim said without looking at me.

"When? Was it before you left Australia?"

"Yes. But I was planning on coming home anyway."

"Well, it all makes sense now. You were coming home to my bank account, not to me."

He reached across the couch and grabbed my hand. "Katie, I love you."

I snatched my hand back. "You love my money. You love that I always take care of everything. You love being babied, first by your mother and your older sisters and then by me. Oh my God, I can't believe I've wasted so much of my life on you. You're a good looking forty-three-year-old child. I hope for your sake, and our daughter's, you manage to grow up some day."

"Katie, wait…"

I stood. "Thank you for your time, Dr. Frank, but I won't be back."

Epilogue

A crash came room the great room. I ran from the kitchen and saw Lucy covered with tinsel, a silver angel ornament in pieces at her feet.

"Mommy, I'm sorry. I didn't mean to break it."

I bent down and hugged her. "Not to worry, sweetie. It's not Christmas if we don't lose an ornament or two. Now go upstairs and put on your new shoes. Our guests will be here any minute."

I walked to the kitchen to get a broom, squeezing past the servers the catering company had provided for the party. I was expecting around forty people, and I wanted everything to be perfect. One of the servers offered to clean up the broken ornament, giving me time to put on some jewelry and fresh lipstick before my guests arrived. I walked up to my bedroom and found the emerald earrings and matching emerald necklace I'd treated myself to for my forty-third birthday last month. The emeralds went perfectly with my black velvet dress.

After that final counseling session, I filed for divorce. Jim made the divorce easy for me. He gave me full custody of Lucy and, to his credit, refused to take a penny of my *Gold Coast Wives* money. The real estate market rebounded somewhat and we sold the house, clearing a small profit. Our portfolio also recovered a bit. Jim used his portion of our assets to buy his uncle's charter boat business. His time in Australia had taught him that he didn't belong behind a desk. Jim moved into a small two bedroom condo not far from Peg's house in East Moriches and recently started dating an attractive blond teacher in her early thirties. I suspect he won't be single for long.

Angela made a killing from her jewelry line, even selling it on QVC. Her pitch shows are hilarious. Deirdre's flash cards were quite successful, and she made enough money to pay off her credit card debt. A national teaching magazine asked her to write a monthly column, which she's very proud of. Gordon is doing well and doesn't seem to miss coaching the soccer Lolitas.

On the Shores of the Shannon was moderately successful, and my mother is hard at work on its sequel, *Streets Paved with Gold*. She and Dad upgraded to a three bedroom villa on a golf course outside of Tampa as their winter home. Uncle Sean and Peg bought a two bedroom model in the same complex and plan to move down there after their wedding in March. Yes, at age seventy two Peg is taking another chance on love. Perhaps I should too.

"You look beautiful." Paul stood in the doorway.

"You don't look so bad yourself." I kissed his cheek, inhaling the subtle musky aftershave I'd bought him last month.

"Is there anything you need me to do before everyone gets here?" Paul asked.

"Could you check the wine?"

"Of course."

Paul, ever the gentleman, had stepped aside once Jim had returned. I called him once it was clear things were over with Jim, but we've both agreed we're better off as friends. At least for now. My heart is bruised, and I think Paul knows this.

In late October I received a call from Martina Campbell, of all people, asking if I would be interested in a general counsel position with one of her clients based in New York but who was opening up a London office. I met with the CEO, a young whiz kid in his late thirties who knew me from the hedge fund seminar circuit and whose wife was a huge fan of the show. I agreed to spend six months in London and expect to return to New York sometime in the summer. I'm looking forward to getting back to work. Being able to spend a short time living in Europe with Lucy is a total bonus.

A contingent of the Griffin cousins--Molly, Dennis, Patrick and Annie--arrived first, with their assorted spouses and children. Next to arrive was my Uncle Danny, followed by my parents, the Rosettis, and several of the dance class yummies and their families. The disparate groups had been mixing nicely when I saw Shari, her husband and their two sons enter the great room.

"Shari! You made it," I said rushing over to her.

"Yeah, and we only got lost twice."

"Come in, come in. Can I get you a drink?"

"Oh, that's what husbands are for. Hon, can you get me a white wine?" she said to her harried husband. "Now let me take a look at you," Shari

Bernadette Walsh

said, giving me an appraising look. "You look good. Happy. Looks like you survived this, kiddo."

"Yeah, by the skin of my teeth." I laughed.

"Well, I'm expecting an invite to London."

"It took you over three years to make it out to Long Island. I'm only going to be in London for six months."

"No offense, London has better shopping than Long Island so there's a better chance I'll make it."

"Like you need to do more shopping. But seriously, I would love it if you came. And even if you don't, we can meet for lunch once I return to the New York office."

"Your offices are on Lex, right?"

"Yeah, we have space in the Bloomberg Building, so Midtown Diner here we come."

Shari smiled. "I'm so there!"

Don arrived, accompanied by his new girlfriend Jill, one of his first wife's bridge partners. I couldn't imagine Jill wearing anything more racy than a cashmere sweater set. Quite a change from Pamela. For someone so recently separated, Don seemed happy and content.

I hadn't spoken to my former cast mates since the reunion show. Tina had rejoined the cast of *Hope's Glen* in early October. Her character Camilla had been completely transformed by her long coma and had become a psychic and mystical presence in the town of Hope's Glen. The show had given her a much younger boyfriend, which I'm sure had made Tina happy.

I hadn't heard much about Rachel, although I'd caught a glimpse of her at a charity cocktail party my new boss had dragged me to the previous month. Of course she hadn't come over to say hello, but she hadn't screamed at me and called me a drunk, either. I guess that's a form of progress.

I heard about Pamela from Paul. After threatening to fight for full custody of their daughter Diana, Pamela had caved and let her spend alternate weeks with Don. On the European leg of her book tour in September, Pamela had met a thrice divorced minor member of the royal family--Lord Fitzsimmons, I believe. Rumor had it, Pamela and the Lord had become very hot and heavy since Diana has been spending most of her time with Don now. If they get married and she becomes Lady Pamela, I am definitely skipping Queen of the Rosary's next reunion.

I entered the den to check on the kids. Lucy was playing with her older cousins and seemed to be having fun. I'd walked back into the kitchen to check on the caterers when I saw my father.

"Hey, it's your party," he said. "What are you doing hiding in the kitchen?"

"I'm not hiding, Dad, I'm just checking everything's okay."

"That's what you're paying these nice ladies for. Stop taking care of everyone else for once and have a good time. You deserve it, hon," he said as he gave my arm a squeeze. "Go join your friends."

I looked out and saw Angela and Jerry entertaining my mother and Deirdre, Shari chatting with Melissa Green from dance class, and Don pouring Gordon a glass of wine. All of these people here to wish me well. In many ways, this night was more precious to me than Encore's millions.

"Everyone," I said. "I would like to make a toast."

They turned to me as my cousin Dennis lowered the music.

"This has been an incredible year. Each of you in your own way has supported me and stuck by me, and for that I will always be grateful. Thank you for coming here tonight, and thank you for your friendship."

Everyone smiled and raised their glasses.

Angela shouted out, "And here's to Kate's next season of *Gold Coast Wives*!"

Season Two? God forbid.

Meet the Author

BIO GOES HERE

Turn the page for a special excerpt of Bernadette Walsh's

The Devlin Witch

You will hate Him for all that he's taken, but you will love Him. God help you, you will love Him.

Mary Devlin accepted her fate years ago, to serve Slanaitheoir, the mountain spirit who saved her ancestors from the Irish Famine. The hauntingly beautiful woman submitted to His every caress, His every humiliation, but He's gone too far by threatening her family.

Mary's daughter-in-law is now an unwitting pawn in the fickle spirit's game. Mary must challenge her fate and that of all future Devlin women, but Slanaitheoir is the most powerful being in the land. And when part of her still yearns for His touch and love, how can she fight him and win?

On sale now!

Chapter 1

Caroline

When the doctors told me I'd never have children, I thought I would die. I thought it was the worst thing that could happen to me.

I was wrong.

But, as I sat on the steps of Old St. Patrick's Cathedral that September afternoon willing my newly straightened hair not to frizz, my only concern was the priest was late, still in with the couple whose wedding was to follow ours. Bobby, effortlessly handsome with his new haircut, squeezed my hand.

I looked at the still unfamiliar Cartier watch Bobby had given me that morning as a wedding gift. "I told the restaurant we'd be there by six."

"We've plenty of time," he said in the soft Dublin brogue that had captivated me seven months earlier.

"But..."

Bobby shut me up me by kissing me on the lips. He smiled. "We've plenty of time."

A group of NYU students sauntered past us, the girls in their skimpy tank tops reveling in summer's last gasp. Bobby stretched out on the church's stone steps, legs spread out like a cat soaking up the sun. He twisted the strange ring on his right hand, a family heirloom shaped like twisted branches. Aside from his mindless twirling of the ring, Bobby looked like he hadn't a care in the world. My mind of course raced with the hundreds of details the wedding entailed. To be honest, organizational skills had never been my strong suit, and I couldn't for the life of me remember whether I sent the final check to the florist.

There was no word from the priest as we wilted in the sun, although I was the only one who minded. My mother, wearing her highest heels and brightest lipstick, chatted with Bobby's father and overdressed stepmother. Bobby's sister, Orla, her hair dyed a particularly aggressive blond, wiped her two-year-old son's face as she and her husband laughed with two of my brothers. I think the Irish relatives, both Bobby's family and my mother's, were happy to have an excuse to make a trip to New York and they seemed to enjoy the West Village street scene. Even my father's family seemed less miserable than usual.

But not my father. He stood apart from everyone and leaned against the church's ornate doors. After more than thirty-five years of marriage, any evidence of my mother's Catholicism and her Irishness still made my Methodist, dyed in the wool WASP father cringe. Being the child of what my mother referred to as a "mixed" marriage, my religious observance over the years was admittedly spotty, but there was no way my mother's only daughter was going to get away without a church wedding. The minute we announced our engagement my mother flew into overdrive and planned the entire thing in two months. When my father grumbled about footing the bill for an extravagant Manhattan wedding, in a Catholic church no less, she told him in her still strong County Kerry accent, "Hush, now, there's no pockets in a shroud."

The priest came out. "Come in, please. I'm sorry I was delayed."

Bobby scanned the street. A fire engine roared past.

"Do you want us to wait for her?" I said over the piercing siren.

His mouth tightened. The siren faded into the distance. "No, no. Let's go in."

I smoothed one of his errant curls. "Maybe her flight was delayed?"

He shrugged, his shoulders slightly hunched. "Maybe."

Bobby's sister Orla came up behind him and took his arm. "Come on now, brother. I told you she wouldn't show. Don't let it ruin your day."

Bobby said nothing as we walked into the church.

Thirty minutes later, after the priest told us where to stand and what to do, our group spilled out of the church and walked the two blocks to the Italian restaurant I'd booked for the rehearsal dinner. I was laughing at Orla's son, Brendan, when a woman walked toward us.

She was tall, slim, with black wavy hair that hung down her back. Her skin was clear with a hint of rose at the cheeks. Her eyes, even from a distance, were an unearthly green. They almost glowed in the late evening sun.

My mother stopped so suddenly I bumped into her. "*Draiodair Mna*," she whispered.

"Ma, what is it?"

She pointed at the woman and then said louder, "*Draiodair Mna.*"

"Ma, what are you saying?"

My normally bossy, confident mother looked at me with the eyes of a terrified child. "The witch. His witch. The Mountain's whore."

I turned to Bobby. "I don't know what's wrong with her. Who is that woman?"

Without looking at me, he said, "That's my mother."

* * * *

We stood there for a moment. It was Brendan who broke the silence by running to the dark-haired woman. "Nana!"

"My little man." She scooped him up into her arms.

Orla quickly took her son from her mother and said in a clipped tone, "So you made it then, Mam."

She kissed Bobby. "Yes, I'm sorry I'm late." She turned to me. "You must be Caroline. I'm pleased to finally meet you."

"Me too." I kissed her cheek.

Behind me my mother growled, "And I'm her mother."

Bobby's mother held out her hand. "Lovely to meet you. I'm Mary Connelly."

"Don't you mean Mary Devlin? Mary Devlin from Devil's Mountain?"

Mary peered into my mother's face. "Nellie? Nellie Collins?"

"Who else? Or are you surprised I'm still alive, not crushed by a bus like my poor Jimmy?"

Mary looked like she'd been slapped. "Nellie, no. I'm surprised is all. It's been a long time."

"Not long enough!"

We blocked the narrow sidewalk and a giggly crowd of students pushed past us. My father held out his hand to Mary. "I'm Caroline's father. We're glad you could join us. Please, the restaurant is right down the street. Let me show you." And with that, my sour, introverted father gallantly offered Mary his arm and led her through the throng of happy hour revelers to the restaurant.

I took my mother's arm. "Come on, Ma. Let's go."

"She's spinning her web already."

"Ma, please. I don't know what's up with you and Bobby's mother but you have to calm down."

She looked up at me. "It's not too late, Caro. You can still call it off."

"Call what off?"

"You can't marry into that family," she said, her voice now trembling. "It will be the death of you."

I dropped her arm. "Cancel the wedding? Are you crazy?"

"Caroline, please. Please listen to me!"

My father's sister turned to look at us. I whispered in my mother's ear, "I've heard enough. For God's sake, get a hold of yourself."

When we reached the restaurant I practically ran to its small bar. As I gulped down my drink, I berated myself for caving into my mother's demand for a big wedding. I was thirty, and in the past two years I'd attended close to twenty weddings. They were boring and expensive and I had more pouffy bridesmaid dresses than I cared to count. A big wedding was the last thing I wanted.

Bobby, too, was hesitant to put his family through the stress of a wedding. From what little he'd said, his parent's divorce three years ago was both unexpected and devastating. Mary had found her husband kissing his secretary in a local pub. It fractured the family, with Orla taking the father's side and Bobby taking the mother's. Bobby's father ran off to London with his secretary for a quickie wedding as soon as the ink was dry on their divorce. Mary, who was stunning, really, and looked years younger than her age and certainly younger than the chubby new wife, had returned to her childhood home in Kerry, to Devlin's Mountain. Bobby was so thrown by it all he'd accepted an offer from an investment bank in New York and emigrated soon thereafter. The four of them--well, I guess five, if you include the new wife--hadn't been in the same room since Bobby left Ireland. The last thing he needed today was my mother's antics.

Tina, my best friend since second grade and maid of honor, joined me at the bar. "Why is your mother crying?"

"Oh, Jesus! I seriously thought I'd kill her last week over the seating chart debacle, but this...this is too much."

"Why? What's going on?"

"I have no idea. Apparently my mother knows Bobby's mother from Ireland and she doesn't seem to like her."

Tina lit a cigarette and ignored the waiter's disapproving look. "Did she say why?"

"She said she's a witch, but you know how my mother likes to exaggerate. Mary probably stole her hair ribbon or tripped her in the schoolyard. She doesn't want me to marry into that family."

"What? I thought your mother was so into the wedding. Too into the wedding, you said."

"Yeah, she was. Now she wants me to cancel it." I held up my martini. "Hence, the need for alcohol."

In the middle of my second drink the maitre d' asked me whether I wanted them to serve the appetizers. "Sure," I said with a sigh, "might as well get this show on the road."

Tina rubbed my arm. "It'll be fine. You know that, right? Every wedding has its hiccups."

"Tina, the florist sent the wrong color flowers at your wedding. My mother's accused the groom's mother of being a witch. Not exactly the same thing."

Tina smiled. "It'll be fine. You'll see."

Ignoring her carefully constructed seating plan, my mother sat as far away from the Connellys as was possible in the small restaurant. The two-piece band Bobby had hired played during dinner and, upon my instructions, the waiters made sure no one's glass was empty. Everyone began to relax. Even Bobby. The strained look he'd worn ever since his mother arrived faded.

In between courses, I circulated among the tables of our friends and relatives. A few of my mother's relatives danced on the makeshift dance floor. As I chatted with my aunt, Dorothy, I thought to myself, "Maybe this won't be so bad. Maybe it will all settle down."

And then I saw her.

My mother had cornered poor Bobby on his way to the bar. From the expression on Bobby's face, it didn't look like they were talking about the food.

Aunt Dorothy was mid-sentence when I stormed over to the bar.

"Bobby, you've been in my house, what, at least a dozen times," I heard my mother say. "I don't understand why you never mentioned your people were from Kilvarren. What were you hiding?"

"Honestly, I never thought of it. I grew up in Dublin. You know that. Sure, everyone in Dublin has family down the country. My father's family is from Roscommon. I didn't tell you that either." Bobby's delivery seemed a bit slick, even to me. His voice had the slightly false bravado I'd only heard him use when he'd taken me to dinner with clients, the same tone I imagined he used when he was trying to close a deal.

My mother's face was scarlet at this point. She grabbed his jacket and hissed, "You're lying. My daughter may buy this, but I'll tell you, my little jackeen, I do not. You knew. You knew that if I knew who your family was, what your mother is, I would never permit my daughter to marry you."

I grabbed my mother's arm. "Permit me? Since when do I need your permission? I'm a grown woman. If you're not careful, Mother, you'll find yourself uninvited to this wedding!"

Aunt Dorothy came up behind me. "Bobby, love, you'll have to excuse us. I think these ladies have a case of wedding jitters. Come on now, girls, let's head to the ladies and fix our makeup. Bobby, dear, could you ever go over and make sure that husband of mine's not boring your poor father to tears?"

With a vise-like grip, Aunt Dorothy dragged me and my mother away. The bathroom door hadn't closed before she lit into my mother. "For God's sake, Nellie, what the hell is going on?"

"Tell her, Dotty. Tell her about that family. About that woman."

"Mary Devlin? Why, she's one of my best customers. She comes in every Tuesday for her groceries. She's a lovely woman."

"What are you talking about?" My mother was crying at this point. "Tell Caroline. Tell her about the Mountain."

"Nellie, would you ever cop onto to yourself? No one believes in those old stories any more. It's 1997. Ireland's changed since you left. It's a different world now."

"It's not that different."

Aunt Dorothy's eyes narrowed. "And how would you know? You haven't been back to Kilvarren since Daddy died."

My mother wiped her eyes. "It's an accursed place, Caro. Ever since the Famine. It's cursed and it's evil and it's ruled by those Devlin women. Look at her. How old does she look to you? If I didn't know better I'd say she wasn't a day over thirty-five. But, Caro, Mary Devlin's five years older than myself. How do you think she got that way? It's His doing. Sure, Dorothy, wasn't Mary's mother the same? I'm telling you, Caroline, if you marry into the Devlin family, you'll rue the day. That, I promise you."

Aunt Dorothy's expression softened and she touched my mother's shoulders. "Nellie, love, how many years has it been? Thirty-five at least. You've a lovely husband, a lovely family. You need to let Jimmy go."

Ignoring her, my mother stared at me. "I know what I know, Caro. If you go through with this, you can't say I didn't warn you."

"I love him, Mama. I don't care--"

The door swung open and little Brendan barreled in, followed by the harried Orla. "Hiya, ladies. What a fantastic place, Caroline. The food is beautiful."

"Thanks. I'm glad you're enjoying yourself."

Orla noted my mother's red eyes. "Oh, sorry, are we interrupting?"

I took my mother's arm. "No, not at all. We're done here, right, Ma?

"Yes," she said in a small voice. "We're done."

The restaurant was hushed as we walked in from the bathroom, with everyone's eyes on the small dance floor. The band played an old Irish love ballad. Bobby's mother and father danced alone. Paul Connolly held Mary close as their bodies swayed to the music, his face buried in Mary's silky black curls. The air was charged with their emotions, making it impossible to look away. The song came to an end. Paul lifted his face out of Mary's curls, tears streaming.

Fiona, Paul's new wife, banged her drink on the table, grabbed a pack of cigarettes and stomped past the couple and out onto the street. Paul didn't notice. His eyes never left Mary's.

* * * *

The air was cool, crisp, and the sky a sparkling clear blue when the limo deposited us outside the church. My father offered me his arm, and smiled even, as we walked up the stone steps.

We were early, the church still quiet, with only the florist there arranging the altar's enormous flower displays. My mother, who seemed reconciled to this wedding going forward, once again became the efficient mother of the bride and led me into a small room off the entranceway to fix my veil, which she told me was crooked, and my lipstick, which she told me was too light.

The florist, who for some reason failed to deliver mine and the bridesmaids' bouquets to my apartment as ordered, had deposited them in this room. My soon-to-be mother-in-law was holding my bouquet in her hands.

"Mary," I said. "What are you doing here?"

"My cab dropped me off early and I thought I'd fix my face before everyone got here. I was looking for the bathroom and I saw these. They are beautiful."

My mother grabbed the bouquet from her. "And the wrong color. I ordered deep blush roses, not pale pink. Oh, Caro, these won't do. These won't do at all!"

"Leave them, Ma. They're fine."

"You look lovely, Caroline," Mary said in her soft, lilting brogue. She touched my veil. "I'm happy I was able to come. My son is a lucky man."

"Thank you, Mary. We're glad you made it," I said, almost meaning it. After her dance with her ex-husband last night, the mood changed. Orla ran after her stepmother, who came back to the restaurant with red eyes.

Orla and Bobby had argued in the corner, my mother and Aunt Dorothy kept disappearing into the ladies room, and Paul had continued to stare at Mary like a lovesick schoolboy, despite Fiona's glares. After dessert was served, guests made their excuses and the rehearsal party had ended more than an hour early. I couldn't help thinking the night would've gone much smoother had Mary stayed up on her mountain.

My mother was a woman possessed as she plucked the deeper pink roses out of the bridesmaids' bouquets and stuck them in my own. She was almost done, when she pulled out a small purple flower.

"What is this, Mary?"

"I, uh..."

"I'll ask you again. What is this?"

"Just a little something for luck, Nellie."

My mother tore through the bouquet. Petals scattered at her feet. "What else, you she-devil? What else did you put in here?"

"Nothing, Nellie. 'Twas nothing."

"Nothing?" My mother held a small mud-colored heart in her palm. "Then, what is this?"

"Please, Nellie," Mary pleaded. "Only a charm. For luck. Please leave it there!"

My mother threw the small heart to the floor and crushed it beneath her new Jimmy Choos. "I've had enough of your charms. I'll not have you interfering with my daughter. Keep your black magic and His evil powers to yourself."

Mary deflated before us, and for the first time, I could almost see her sixty years in her green eyes. "I meant no harm. Truly, I didn't. I'll leave you now."

Without another word, my mother reconstructed the bouquets and they were almost as good as new. She fixed my lipstick and my veil. I was ready to go.

Years later, I'd often wonder what would've happened if my mother hadn't disturbed Mary's charms.